D1579697

Every family ... , the secrets stay b... ...ey rise up out of the pa... ...g sh...w. across the present. What do you do then? Is it better to look the other way, and 'let sleeping dogs lie'?

Brat Farrar is a quiet, serious young man, who has never done anything criminal before. He has no intention of becoming an imposter, of pretending to be Patrick Ashby and inheriting the Ashby house and fortune. Why does he change his mind? Is it the money, or is it the challenge, the excitement? It would be quite easy to pretend to be the dead Patrick Ashby, and then he would have an easy, comfortable life . . .

But it was not so simple, after all. After a time, the new Patrick Ashby began to feel sorry for the boy who had killed himself all those years ago. And then he began to wonder about the past, which is sometimes a dangerous thing to do.

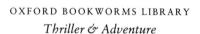

OXFORD BOOKWORMS LIBRARY

Thriller & Adventure

Brat Farrar

Stage 5 (1800 headwords)

Series Editor: Jennifer Bassett
Founder Editor: Tricia Hedge
Activities Editors: Jennifer Bassett and Alison Baxter

JOSEPHINE TEY

Brat Farrar

Retold by
Ralph Mowat

OXFORD UNIVERSITY PRESS

OXFORD
UNIVERSITY PRESS

Great Clarendon Street, Oxford OX2 6DP

Oxford University Press is a department of the University of Oxford.
It furthers the University's objective of excellence in research, scholarship,
and education by publishing worldwide in

Oxford New York

Auckland Cape Town Dar es Salaam Hong Kong Karachi
Kuala Lumpur Madrid Melbourne Mexico City Nairobi
New Delhi Shanghai Taipei Toronto

With offices in

Argentina Austria Brazil Chile Czech Republic France Greece
Guatemala Hungary Italy Japan Poland Portugal Singapore
South Korea Switzerland Thailand Turkey Ukraine Vietnam

OXFORD and OXFORD ENGLISH are registered trade marks of
Oxford University Press in the UK and in certain other countries

Original edition © 1949 by Elizabeth MacKintosh
First published by Peter Davies 1949
The publishers are grateful to William Heinemann Ltd
for permission to create this simplified edition
This simplified edition © Oxford University Press 2008

Database right Oxford University Press (maker)

First published in Oxford Bookworms 1992

12 14 16 18 20 19 17 15 13 11

No unauthorized photocopying

ISBN 978 0 19 479217 2

Printed in China

ACKNOWLEDGEMENTS
Illustrated by: Mike Allport

Word count (main text): 24,510 words

For more information on the Oxford Bookworms Library,
visit www.oup.com/bookworms

CONTENTS

Chapter One

The Ashby family

'Why can't you eat more politely, Jane? Like your sister Ruth!' said Bee across the lunch table.

'She's better at spaghetti than I am, that's all,' said Jane. 'I can't be bothered with things like that.'

Her Aunt Bee looked along the table at the twins Jane and Ruth, and smiled. They were almost ten, and were exactly the same, but it was never difficult to tell which was Jane and which was Ruth. Jane always seemed to wear old clothes, clothes for riding horses and for working with them. Ruth, on the other hand, was always in a fresh, clean dress, her hands were never dirty and her hair was always neat and tidy.

Eight years, thought Bee. Eight years since the sudden, shocking death of the twins' mother and father, Nora and Bill, in that terrible plane crash! Eight years since she left her life and her job in London to come to Latchetts in order to look after her dead brother's children. And soon she would no longer be responsible for them. The twins' brother, Simon, would be twenty-one in a few weeks' time, and his mother's fortune would be his. The father had not been poor; the Ashby family had lived comfortably at Latchetts for more than two hundred years, but they had never been rich. Latchetts was a small estate of three farms, the park and the house itself. Bill's death had left his sister Bee with many problems as well as those of bringing up his children. Bee had refused to use the money that had belonged to Bill's wife, and had been determined to manage the estate as a successful business. The money would go to the oldest son when he was twenty-one and Bee had decided not to touch it. So Latchetts had earned its living as a farm for horses, as a school for training horses, as a school for people who

1

wanted to learn to ride, and each year Latchetts had made a profit. Bee had made sure of that.

And in six weeks' time Simon would be twenty-one, would receive his mother's money, and become master of Latchetts. What would he do with it, wondered Bee, as she watched his fair head across the lunch table.

Simon, who had so much charm, but who was also so selfish. He seemed so often to want help, but always with such a charming manner that people helped him, even before he asked. In fact, it wasn't true that he was helpless; it was just his way of making sure that he could get what he wanted. Unfortunately, very few people, except Bee, seemed to understand this side of Simon's character.

The twins' older sister, Eleanor, came in.

'Oh, you smell of horses,' said Ruth, turning up her nose.

'What made you so late, Eleanor?' asked Bee.

'Oh, the Parslow girl from Clare. But it's a waste of time trying to teach her. She'll never learn to ride.'

'Perhaps mad people can't ride,' suggested Ruth.

'Ruth!' said Bee firmly. 'The pupils at the school at Clare are not crazy. They're just . . . difficult.'

'Well, they seem to be mad, from what I see of them,' answered Ruth.

Silence fell on the Ashby table. Bee thought about Latchetts, the estate that would belong to Simon in a few weeks. She hoped he would look after it well. It was the only local estate to have stayed in the same family for over two hundred years. Even the big estate at Clare, with its beautiful, long, white house had been sold. The Ledingham family had wasted their money and had not looked after their land. In the end they had had to sell the house where they had lived for so long, but which had perhaps never really been a home for them. The house at Clare had become a school for difficult children with rich parents, and the Ledinghams had gone.

But the Ashbys stayed at Latchetts.

As Bee thought about the past, and wondered about the future at Latchetts, the twins finished their meal and went off to play. Eleanor drank her coffee quickly and went back to her horses. Simon was on his way out of the dining-room when a voice in the hall called,

'Bee, are you there?'

'It's Mrs Peck,' said Simon, going out to meet her.

'Come in, Nancy,' called Bee. 'Come and have coffee with me. The others have drunk theirs too quickly, and have rushed off.'

Nancy Peck was the wife of the local priest. Before her marriage she had been Nancy Ledingham of Clare House, a beautiful and famous young woman. Photographs of her used to appear regularly in the national newspapers, and everyone expected her to find a rich, or even a royal, husband. Then, quite suddenly, she had married George Peck, a quiet, gentle country priest. That had been thirteen years ago, and Nancy Peck was still beautiful and still very happily married.

'I'd love some coffee,' said Nancy. 'Some people need whisky to make the world seem better; for me, coffee is better – and no one says it's wrong to drink it. By the way, how are the preparations for Simon's party coming on?'

'Very well. I'm just about to send out the invitations. That reminds me. Your brother, Alec – what's his latest address in London?'

'I can't remember,' replied Nancy. 'He changes flats so often – whenever he can't pay his rent. He's not a very good actor, and I think he's finding it difficult to get work in the theatre. In fact, he's never been successful at anything. You don't know how lucky you are, Bee.'

'What do you mean?' said Bee in a puzzled voice.

3

'I don't mean just you, Bee. I mean the Ashby family. The men in your family are all sensible, good men. Look at my family – most of them in the last fifty years have been stupid, mad, or bad. You don't have anyone like that. The Ashbys are very, very lucky.'

'There was my cousin, Walter,' said Bee.

'Oh, but he wasn't bad. He drank too much, and he was rather silly, but he wasn't bad. All the bad ones around here seem to have been Ledinghams, and Alec is the most recent of them. But don't let's talk about him. I've been thinking of Bill and Nora. This would have been such a happy time for them.'

'Yes,' said Bee quietly. She looked out of the window and remembered the day it had happened. Waiting for her brother and his wife to return from their trip to Europe; the excited children at an upstairs window watching for their parents' car. Without thinking what she was doing, Bee had turned on the radio to hear the news. And then she had heard the words which her head at first refused to believe:

The two o'clock plane from Paris crashed this afternoon. Everyone on the plane was killed.

'Bill and Nora loved the children so much,' Nancy said. 'They would have been so happy for Simon's twenty-first birthday.'

'I've been thinking a lot about Patrick, too,' said Bee sadly.

'Patrick?' Nancy sounded surprised. 'Oh yes, of course. Poor Patrick!'

Bee looked at her friend curiously.

'You had almost forgotten, hadn't you?'

'Well, it's a long time ago, Bee. Patrick's death is something everyone tries to forget. I can't really remember what he looked like any more. Was he as like Simon as Ruth is like Jane?'

'No, they weren't the same, although they were twins. They were very different – in appearance and in character. But they

4

did lots of things together.'

'Simon seems to have put it out of his head. Do you think he remembers Patrick often? It's a long time from twelve to twenty. Even a twin becomes like a shadow after eight years.'

Nancy's remark made Bee stop and think. What could she remember of Patrick – the twin brother, only twenty minutes older than Simon, who would have inherited Latchetts in a few weeks' time? He had been small and fair, similar to other Ashbys, and she remembered him as a quiet, serious young boy. That was really all she could remember now. What had happened to her memories of Patrick, who had died so many years ago?

'That body they found in the sea,' said Bee, unhappily. 'How could they be so sure it was Patrick? It had been in the water for months.'

'But Bee, it must have been Patrick. Nobody else had thrown himself, or fallen, from a cliff near here. I'm sure it was Patrick. And the note was certainly from him.'

'Yes, Nancy,' replied Bee, 'but I don't think he jumped from the cliff. His jacket, with the note, was near the path that goes down to the beach near Westover. I think he swam out to sea until he was too tired to come back. He told me once that would be the best way to die. He loved the water.'

She was silent for a minute, and then told her friend the secret fear she had hidden for so many years.

'I've always been afraid that he changed his mind about what he was doing, but only when it was too late to come back.'

'Oh Bee, no! What a frightening thought! I'm sure it wasn't like that. Patrick was deeply unhappy after his parents' death, and confused and worried because Latchetts suddenly belonged to him. It was all too much for him, and he was so miserable that he . . . took a way out.'

'Perhaps you're right. It seems a long time ago. Let's get back to the present and Simon's party. You won't forget to give me your brother's address, will you?'

'No, I'll look it up as soon as I get back home. But remember, he's Alec Loding in the theatre, not Alec Ledingham. It's a long time since he came to Clare; he doesn't really like the country. But an Ashby twenty-first birthday, that's something special. That's sure to interest him.'

Chapter Two

Alec Loding's plan

But Alec Loding's main interest in an Ashby twenty-first birthday was to stop the party completely. And that was what he was trying to do as he sat in The Green Man pub in London, talking to the young man he had met by chance in the street.

'Well?' said Loding.

'No!' said the young man. 'I'm not an actor.'

'You don't have to act. You look exactly like young Simon Ashby. And it's eight years since his twin brother, Patrick, died. Things change, people change. You'd only have to walk in, and everyone would believe that you were Patrick.'

'It's a crazy idea. Nobody would believe me.'

'Look, I'm offering you a fortune. Just to be yourself.'

'Half a fortune. You want the other half. And you're not offering me anything. You're suggesting a criminal plan between the two of us to cheat this Simon Ashby out of his estate and his money.'

'What are you afraid of, Farrar? You look so like Simon that I thought for a moment that you really were young Ashby. Isn't that good enough for you? Come and live with me for a fortnight, and by the end of it you'll know everything there is

'*I'm not an actor.*'

to know about the village of Clare, Latchetts and the Ashby family.'

'I doubt it,' replied the young man.

'But your story would be so easy. Except for the first year or so, your real life would be the truth. People could check as much as they liked. It's only the beginning you have to invent. You can say you ran away and hid on a ship going to France.'

'I don't like the idea. I'm not that kind of person. But thank you very much for my lunch. If I'd known why you were asking me to have lunch with you, I wouldn't have . . .'

'All right, all right,' said Loding. 'But think about it. Why not come and look at my photographs of the house and family? I'll give you my address, in case you change your mind.'

'I don't think I shall,' replied the young man, 'but I'll take your address.'

'Here you are, then. I'm really sorry I couldn't sell you the idea of being an Ashby. I feel you would have been an excellent master of Latchetts. Someone who knew all about horses and was used to an outdoor life.'

The young man was about to walk out of the pub, but stopped suddenly.

'Horses, did you say?'

'Yes,' said Loding, surprised. 'Latchetts is a stud. Didn't I mention that? They breed horses. I believe they're very well known.'

'Oh,' said the young man, and went off down the street.

That night the young man lay on his bed in the dark, fully dressed, and stared at the ceiling. He was thinking about the past, the journey through life that had brought him to this small room in London. He had always been alone in life. It had disturbed him to find that somewhere there was another young man so like him that they could be mistaken for one another. Indeed, it was the most surprising thing that had happened to him in all his twenty-one years. That moment when a man stopped in the street and greeted him.

'Hello, Simon.'

'Oh! Sorry!' the man said at once. 'Thought you were a friend of mine, but . . .' And then he had stopped and stared.

'Can I do something for you?' the boy had asked.

'Yes. You could come and have lunch with me.'

'Why?'

'Because you interest me. You are so like a friend of mine. My name is Loding, by the way. I'm an actor, but not a very successful one. Do you mind telling me your name?'

'Farrar.'

'Oh! Is it long since you came back to England?' asked Loding.

'How did you know I had been out of it?'

'Your clothes, my boy. They're my business, and I can recognize American clothes without any difficulty.'

So they had gone to lunch and Loding had talked about the man who looked so much like Farrar.

And now he, Brat Farrar, lay on his bed and thought about it. He suddenly had a strong wish to see this twin of his, this Ashby boy. And 'Latchetts' – a nice English name for a place. It sounded very different to the life he had known, a life in which he had never been close to anyone and had never known any family. Life in the orphanage had not been bad. He had been left on the doorstep when he was a baby. No one knew who his parents were and his name had been chosen out of the telephone book. He had stayed there for fifteen years, until he was old enough to go out and work. He had hated the office where he worked, and one day he had left, bought a day ticket to Dieppe and never returned. He had planned to stay and work in France, but he had no official papers, so he took a job on an old ship, and went to Mexico. After that he had many jobs as he worked

9

his way north through Mexico and into the United States.

It was in the States that he had his first job with horses and found real happiness. He was good with horses, especially the ones that were difficult to train, and over the next few years he earned quite good money. He had his own beautiful horse, called Smoky, but then came his accident. A horse rolled on top of him and his leg was broken. When he came out of hospital, one leg was shorter than the other and he was lame. Smoky had gone and Brat was sad again, but he continued to make money at his next job in a riding school.

One day he realized that he wanted to see England again. He had enough money for the journey, and so here he was in this little back room in London, thinking about Alec Loding, Latchetts and horses. Brat got up and walked around his small bedroom. Why hadn't he been shocked? As soon as Loding had started talking to him, Brat had realized that some dishonest idea would be coming. Loding was so obviously that kind of person.

Brat thought about the future. He had no job, and good jobs with horses were not easy to find. What could he do? He wanted to work with horses, and he knew now that he liked England and wanted to stay. But Loding's plan was criminal, and he wouldn't have anything to do with that.

'It would be quite safe, you know,' said a quiet voice inside him.

'Shut up,' he replied. 'It would be wrong.'

'Loding's a clever man,' said the voice. 'You look so like an Ashby, you must be one. So what's wrong in having some of their money? They'd probably want to help you.'

'No, they wouldn't. There's no reason why they should. And Loding may be very clever, but he's also bad. I don't want to have anything to do with him.'

'You're throwing away the chance of a lifetime,' complained

the voice. 'And you'd be working with horses, English horses, remember.'

'Shut up. You're wasting your time,' replied Brat angrily, but he was still curious to see what his 'twin' looked like. Perhaps he should go and look at the photographs that Loding had talked about.

That would do no harm, and he could see what Latchetts looked like.

'That's better,' said the voice happily. 'Let's go tomorrow.'

Chapter 3

Back from the dead

It was the end of a long London afternoon and Mr Sandal, lawyer to many respectable families, was about to leave his office when his secretary told him that there was another visitor waiting to see him.

'It's young Mr Ashby,' she said.

'Ashby? Of Latchetts?' he asked.

'Yes, sir.'

'Oh good. Show him in.'

The young man came in.

'Ah, Simon. I'm delighted to see you. Are you in London on business, or are you just . . .'

His voice hesitated, uncertain, and he stared at the young man who had just walked into his office.

'But,' he frowned, 'you are not Simon.'

'No. I'm not Simon.'

'But – you are an Ashby,' said Mr Sandal, continuing to stare at his visitor.

'If you think that, it makes things much easier for me,'

11

replied the young man.

'I'm sorry. I don't really understand. I didn't know that there were any Ashby cousins.'

'There aren't, as far as I know.'

'No? Then which Ashby are you?'

'Patrick.'

Mr Sandal's mouth fell open, and he stared even more closely at his visitor.

'I think we had better both sit down,' he said at last. 'Now, let us try to get this clear. The only Patrick Ashby died at the age of thirteen, almost eight years ago.'

'What makes you think he died?'

'He killed himself and left a note to say "Goodbye".'

'Did the note say anything about killing himself?' asked the young man.

'I can't remember the exact words,' replied Mr Sandal.

'Nor can I, exactly. But I remember the general meaning. It said: "I can't bear it any longer. Don't be angry with me." That doesn't say anything about killing himself, does it?'

'But the letter was found at the top of the cliffs, in the pocket of the boy's jacket. That clearly suggests what he was going to do,' argued the lawyer.

'From the top of the cliffs there is a path which is a short way down to the harbour.'

'The harbour? You mean —'

'Patrick was running away. That's what the note meant. He didn't kill himself,' said the young man calmly.

'Are you seriously telling me that – that you are Patrick Ashby, and that you did not die in the sea eight years ago?' said Mr Sandal in a worried voice.

The young man looked at him with those clear eyes which showed nothing at all of his feelings. 'When I came in,' he said, 'you thought it was my brother.'

'Yes. I suppose I did. Simon and Patrick were twins, and you certainly look . . .' Mr Sandal stopped suddenly as he began to realize the full meaning of his visitor's words. 'You must understand,' he went on after a moment, 'that I cannot simply accept that what you say is true without much more information. And everything will have to be most carefully investigated.'

'I understand,' replied the young man.

'For example, when you ran away, where did you go? I suppose you ran away to sea. What was the name of the ship you left on?'

'The *Ira Jones*. She was in Westover that day.'

'You hid on the ship, I suppose. And no one saw you.'

'That's right.'

'And where did the ship take you?' asked the lawyer.

'To the Channel Islands.'

'And what did you do then?'

'I got a boat to St Malo and I got a job for a few weeks. Helping in the garage of a hotel.'

'Do you remember the name of the hotel?'

'It was the *Dauphin*, in a place called Villedieu. After that I went to Le Havre and worked on a ship that was leaving harbour. I didn't have a passport, you see. That made it difficult to stay in France.'

'The name of the ship? Can you remember?'

'I'll never forget it! She was called the *Barfleur*. I called myself Farrar. F-a-r-r-a-r. We went to Mexico, and then to the United States. Would you like me to write down for you the places where I worked in the States?'

'That would be very kind of you. And when did you come back to England?'

'On the 2nd of last month. On the *Philadelphia*. As a passenger. I rented a room in London, and have lived there ever since.'

'Have you written or spoken to your – I mean – to Miss Ashby?'

'No. I thought it was best to come to you first.'

'That was very sensible. I shall investigate everything you have told me, but I must also say that I cannot understand why you have never communicated with your family before now. Your disappearance caused very deep sadness to many people.'

'Perhaps I liked being dead,' said the young man. 'In any case, you never could understand me very well, could you?'

'Couldn't I?' replied the lawyer, puzzled.

'That day at the horse-show at Olympia, you thought I cried because I was afraid, didn't you?'

'Olympia?'

'I wasn't afraid, you know. I cried because the horses were so beautiful.'

'Olympia!' Memories of a visit long ago with the Ashby family began to come back into Mr Sandal's memory. 'You mean – you remember that day . . . but that was . . .'

'A long time ago. I expect you'll let me know, Mr Sandal, when you've checked everything I've written down.'

Before Mr Sandal could recover from this latest surprise, the young man had gone.

As Brat walked down the street, he was shocked at the feeling of excitement inside him. He had expected to feel rather ashamed, but his visit to Mr Sandal had, in fact, been one of the most exciting experiences he had ever had.

Loding had told him to go to a restaurant, have a meal and watch to see if anyone was following him. Later he went to a telephone.

'Well?' said Loding. 'How did it go?'

'Wonderful! At first the lawyer thought I was Simon.'

Loding laughed. 'What's he going to do now?'

'I've given him a list of everything I did in the States and he's going to check it all very carefully.'

'Well, all that's true, anyway. Do you think he believed you?' Loding wanted to know.

'I think he wasn't sure at first. When I mentioned the children's party at Olympia, he was really surprised. That was when I left. He was still trying to work out how I could possibly know all that if I wasn't Patrick.'

'What a wonderful moment to leave!' The actor in Loding was full of admiration for the young man he had trained to become Patrick Ashby. 'Now, we mustn't meet for some time. It would be too dangerous. I've taught you everything I can, so you're on your own now. Good luck!'

Loding was right. For a fortnight they had sat at different places in Kew Gardens from early morning till seven in the evening. Brat had learned the histories of Ashbys and Ledinghams, the geography of Latchetts and the surrounding countryside, and everything else Loding could remember about Simon and Patrick Ashby. Brat had been a good pupil, and Loding was an excellent teacher. Everything had been learned down to the last detail.

As Brat went home that evening, full of the excitement of the interview with Mr Sandal, he thought to himself: 'There's no going back now.' The voice that had talked to him so often, trying to persuade him to accept Loding's plan, had finally won.

Chapter 4

Breaking the news

The news from Mr Sandal turned Bee's world upside-down. After the telephone call she sat for a long time thinking, wondering, and then went to look for photographs of Patrick. She seemed to have kept nothing at all; some people seem to keep photographs for years and years, but Bee was not one of them. She went to the room that Patrick and Simon had once shared, but she knew very well that nothing of Patrick remained there. Some months after Patrick's death she had found Simon making a fire in the garden. Burning on the fire were Patrick's toys, his schoolbooks, even the silly wooden horse that had hung at the end of his bed. Simon had been very angry when he noticed her watching him.

'I don't want them around,' he had shouted.

'I understand, Simon,' she had said gently and gone away.

The day after the phone call she went to see Mr Sandal.

'Do you believe, yourself, that it is Patrick?' she asked.

'He doesn't seem like an imposter,' replied the lawyer. 'And if he isn't Patrick, then who is he? He looks very like an Ashby.'

'But Patrick would have written,' she said. That was the thought that had stopped her so often in the last twenty-four hours. Patrick would not have left her so upset, so uncertain, for all those years. Therefore, it couldn't be Patrick.

'You're the person who knew Patrick best,' said Mr Sandal. 'You will be the best judge. Simon was only a boy eight years ago, and boys forget.'

So the responsibility was being put on her, thought Bee. How, she wondered, would she know if it was really Patrick?

'But if I'm not sure? What will happen if I'm not sure?' she asked.

16

'We shall have to check every detail of his story very, very carefully.'

'So there's no point in waiting before I see him. How soon can you arrange for me to meet him?'

'I should like us to go and meet him in his room, without warning that we are coming. You'll see him as he is then, and not as he wants you to see him. If I tell him to come to my office, it wouldn't be the same, would it?'

'No. I understand. I think that's a good idea. Can we go now?' asked Bee.

'I don't see why not. He may not be there, but we can go and see.'

Half an hour later Bee and Mr Sandal were climbing the dark stairs that led to Brat Farrar's rented room. Mr Sandal knocked loudly at the door.

'Come in!' said a voice. It was a boy's voice, but rather deep, not at all like Simon's softer way of speaking.

Bee's first feeling on seeing the young man who was inside the room was one of shock – shock that he was so much more like Simon than Patrick had ever been as a child. She had been trying to remember Patrick, and now here was someone who was just like Simon.

The boy did not look bothered or even surprised to see them. He got up from the bed where he had been sitting and said, 'Good morning.'

'Good morning,' said Mr Sandal. 'I hope you don't mind. I've brought you a visitor. Do you know who this is?'

Bee's heart beat a little faster as the boy looked at her calmly.

'You do your hair differently,' he said.

'You recognize her, then?' said Mr Sandal.

'Yes, of course. It's Aunt Bee.'

She waited for him to come forward to greet her, but instead he turned to find a chair for her.

17

'It's Aunt Bee.'

'Miss Ashby could not wait for a meeting at my office, so I brought her here,' Mr Sandal said. 'You don't seem very pleased to . . .' He did not finish.

The boy looked at Bee in a friendly way, but did not smile.

'I'm not very sure if I'm welcome,' he said quietly.

In the silence that followed he walked across the room and she saw that he was lame.

'Have you hurt your leg?' she asked.

'I broke it. Over in the States. It doesn't hurt. It's just short,' the boy replied.

'Short! You mean it will always be like that?'

'It looks like it.'

'But something can be done about that,' said Bee. 'It just means that it mended badly. I expect you didn't have a very good doctor.'

'I don't remember a doctor. But I suppose they did all the correct things.'

'But Pat . . .' she began, and failed to finish his name.

In the silence that followed he said, 'You don't have to call me anything until you're sure.'

'Well, we must see what can be done about your leg,' said Bee, trying to cover her break. 'How did it happen? A horse, was it? You told Mr Sandal that you had worked with horses. Did you enjoy that?'

'It's the only life I do enjoy,' said the young man.

Bee began to hope very much that this was Patrick.

Mr Sandal spoke again. 'Even if Miss Ashby is prepared to recognize you as her nephew, you will understand that the matter must be very fully investigated. This is not just the return of a lost boy to his family. It is also a matter of property and a fortune.'

'I understand perfectly. I shall, of course, stay here until your investigations are finished and you have decided,' said the young man in his deep, calm voice.

So Mr Sandal began his investigations and Bee went back to Latchetts to think about the many problems ahead. The first was to decide how to put off the coming-of-age party without saying why. Mr Sandal did not want her to say anything to Simon and the children yet. If he found out that the young man was not really Patrick, they need never know anything about it.

The person who solved the problem was her Uncle Charles, who had lived abroad for many years. He wrote from Hong Kong to say that he was finally coming home, and he hoped that Simon's party would not take place until he arrived. As Uncle

Charles refused to fly, and always travelled by ship, he would not be in England for several weeks. Uncle Charles was the oldest member of the Ashby family and was also very popular with the children. Everybody thought it was right to wait for his return, and so the date of Simon's party was put off until Uncle Charles could be with them.

Bee was thankful for this way of solving her immediate problem, but her thoughts at this time were very confused. She wanted this boy to be Patrick, but she knew that it would be much better for everyone in the family if, in the end, Mr Sandal proved that he was not Patrick. She wanted Patrick back, warm and alive and dear to her, but she also worried about the enormous problems that would be caused in the happy Ashby family if Patrick really came back.

During these weeks Mr Sandal reported from time to time on his investigations. So far everything seemed to prove that the boy's story was true.

Finally the day came when Mr Sandal informed Bee that the investigations had been completed. He was now officially ready to recognize the boy as Patrick Ashby, the oldest son of William Ashby of Latchetts.

So the moment had come when Bee had to break the news to her family. She decided to tell them when they were all together – after lunch one Sunday.

'I have something to tell you that will be rather a shock to you. But a nice kind of shock,' she said. And she went on from there. Patrick had not killed himself, as they had thought. He had run away. And now he had come back. He had been living in London for several weeks because, of course, he had to prove to the lawyers that he was Patrick. But he had had no difficulty in doing that. And now he was going to come home.

While she was speaking to them, Bee had not looked at their faces; it was easier to talk without seeing their eyes. But in the shocked silence that followed her story she looked across at Simon, and for a moment she did not recognize him. This deathly white face with the burning eyes was not the Simon she knew. She looked away quickly.

'Does it mean that this new brother will get all the money that is Simon's?' asked Jane, in her usual plain way of speaking.

Eleanor said coldly, 'I think it was a horrible thing to do. He left us without a word for – for – how long is it? Seven years? Nearly eight years. And then comes back one day without warning, and expects us to welcome him. It was a horrible thing to do.'

'Is he nice?' said Ruth.

For once Bee was glad of Ruth's interest in other people. 'Yes, he seems to be very nice,' she said.

'How often have you seen him, Aunt Bee?' Eleanor asked.

'Just once. A few weeks ago.'

'Why didn't you tell us about it then?'

'I thought it was better to wait until the lawyers were finished with him and he was ready to come home. It wouldn't have been right for you all to rush off to London to see him, would it?' replied Bee.

'No, I suppose not,' said Eleanor. 'But I expect Simon would have liked to go and see him, wouldn't you, Simon? After all, Patrick was Simon's twin.'

'I don't believe for one moment that it is Patrick,' Simon said in a very careful, cold voice.

Bee sat in unhappy silence. This was even worse than she had expected. 'But Aunt Bee has seen him, Simon. She must know,' said Eleanor. 'And Mr Sandal has accepted him as Patrick.'

'I don't see what possible reason anyone can have for believing that this person is Patrick,' said Simon bluntly.

'Well, for one thing,' said Bee, 'he looks exactly like you. Even more like you now than when he went away.'

'*I don't believe for one moment that it is Patrick.*'

It was obvious that Simon had not expected this.

'Exactly like me?' he repeated rather stupidly and looking very confused.

'Believe me, Simon dear,' said Bee gently, 'it *is* Patrick.'

'It *isn't*. I *know* it isn't. He's playing a trick on all of you. What has this person been doing all these years?'

'He went to Mexico. But first he left Westover on a ship called the *Ira Jones*.'

'Westover? Who says so?'

'He does. And the captain of Westover harbour says that a ship called the *Ira Jones* did leave Westover on the night that Patrick went away.'

Simon stared at her wordlessly. Bee went on.

'Everything he did from then on has been checked – where he worked in France, the ship he sailed on to Mexico, the jobs he had in America . . . all the way back to England. Till the day he walked into Mr Sandal's office.'

'It *isn't* Patrick,' repeated Simon angrily.

'I know it's a shock for you, Simon, my dear,' said Bee. 'But I think you'll find it easier when you see him. He looks so very much an Ashby, and so very like you.'

'When is he coming to Latchetts, Aunt Bee?' asked Eleanor.

'On Tuesday. Unless you want to wait a little, to get more used to the idea.' She turned to Simon, who was looking sick and completely lost.

'If you think that I shall grow used to the idea, you are wrong,' said Simon. 'For me this person is not Patrick, and he never will be.'

And he walked out of the room.

23

Chapter 5

Difficult times

Later that day Bee walked across the fields to visit Nancy and George Peck. Her official reason was to tell them the news of Patrick's return. Her real reason, however, was to talk quietly about Patrick and Simon with George Peck, who was the local priest and a very helpful person to talk to. She found him in the garden looking at flowers. She stood quietly near him, trying to think of what to say.

'George,' she said at last, 'you remember Patrick, don't you?'

'Pat Ashby? Of course.' He turned to look at her.

'Well, he didn't die at all. He just ran away. That's what the note meant. And he's coming back. And Simon isn't pleased.'

George Peck saw a large tear running down her face. 'Come and sit down, Bee,' he said gently, 'and tell me all about it.'

So she told him everything that had happened in the last weeks, and finally the effect of the news on the members of the family.

'Eleanor is cold about it, but she is a reasonable person, and she will accept it. Jane is angry and sorry for Simon, but when she meets her brother she will come to accept him. It's her nature to be friendly.'

'And Ruth?' asked George.

'Ruth is planning what she should wear when Patrick returns.'

The priest smiled. 'People like Ruth are the happy ones in the world.'

'But George, what about Simon? Why is he so angry? It's his twin brother who's coming back.'

'I don't think that's too difficult to understand. For eight years Simon has believed that Latchetts belonged to him. He has

24

known that when he was twenty-one, he would receive his mother's money. Suddenly, without any warning, all that is going to be taken away from him. It's only natural for him to be unhappy about it.'

'I suppose I did it badly – the way I told them. I should have told Simon first. I just didn't think that he would refuse to believe that Patrick is alive.'

'Perhaps that's only his way of pushing the unwelcome fact away from him. You're an adult, and you remember Patrick. You loved him and are happy that he's alive. Simon was a child – he cannot really remember Patrick, and so he has no real love to help him accept Patrick's return. This is just someone coming to take away from him everything that belonged to him.'

'Oh George,' said Bee, 'I didn't think of it like that.'

'It's going to be very difficult for Simon. But this does explain something that has puzzled me for eight years. I could never understand why Patrick killed himself. Patrick was a very sensible child with a great sense of responsibility, and I could never really believe that he could take his own life. It was so unlike him. But tell me, Bee, are you pleased with this adult Patrick who has come back?'

'Yes. Yes, I am pleased. He is in some ways very like the Patrick who went away. And he still loves horses.'

'That will make you happy,' George said with a smile.

'Yes,' agreed Bee. 'It's good that Latchetts should go to someone who really loves horses. To Simon, horses are useful, important, but he has no real feeling for them.'

As Bee walked back to Latchetts, she was thinking of what George Peck had said about Patrick – 'a child with a great sense of responsibility'. And that had been the Patrick that she, too, had remembered. But that Patrick would have written to them. So why hadn't he written?

At about the same time, Brat Farrar was on the point of

changing his mind.

Mr Sandal had given him the money to buy a new suit, but looking at himself in the mirror had been a shock. How had he got himself into this situation? How could he go on with Loding's criminal plan?

He couldn't do it, that was all, he decided. He just couldn't do it. He would stop now, before it was too late.

'What?' said the voice inside him. 'Turn down the greatest adventure of your life? And leave a fortune behind?'

'Yes,' Brat replied. 'Who wants a fortune anyway?'

'And forget about the chance of owning a stud? And never even see Latchetts at all?' went on the voice.

Brat tried to think of an answer.

'If you stop now, you won't get a second chance.'

'But what has Latchetts to do with me?' said Brat.

'You ask that? You look like an Ashby. You're accepted as an Ashby. And you know inside that you really are an Ashby. Don't pretend that you don't care about Latchetts,' insisted the voice.

'I didn't say I didn't care. Of course I care. But I can't do something that is criminal,' replied Brat angrily.

'Can't you? What have you been doing for the last few weeks? And you've been enjoying it. You've loved telling lies that people believe. Don't start getting frightened now! You know that you want to live at Latchetts as an Ashby. You want horses. You want adventure. You want a life in England. Go to Latchetts on Tuesday, and they are all yours,' the voice went on cleverly.

Brat had no answer to that. He sat on the edge of the bed, his face buried in his hands. He was still sitting there when darkness came.

Chapter Six

Welcome home?

It was a beautiful day, the day that Brat Farrar came to Latchetts, but there was a little wind that made people feel uncertain of the weather and wonder if a storm was on its way.

Bee had worried a lot about Brat's arrival. It should be as simple as possible, but who was to meet the new brother at the station and bring him home, to Latchetts? Ruth and Jane thought that everyone should go, but Bee knew that would be wrong. Simon clearly wanted to have nothing to do with the new Patrick, so Bee was a little surprised, but also very pleased, when Eleanor offered to drive to the station and bring Patrick back.

Her next worry was about lunch, the first meal after Patrick's arrival. What if Simon didn't come home for lunch? And if he did, what would happen?

Guessgate was a small station and Brat was the only person who got off the train that morning.

'Hullo,' said Eleanor. 'You're very like Simon.'

Brat noticed that this girl who had met him was wearing everyday clothes and had obviously been riding.

'Eleanor,' he said.

'Yes, that's right. Where's the rest of your luggage?'

'This is all I've got,' said Brat, pointing at his small case.

'Been away, Mr Ashby?' said the man who collected Brat's ticket as they came out of the station.

'Yes, I've been away,' replied Brat, and at the sound of his voice the man looked up, puzzled.

'He thought you were Simon,' Eleanor said with a smile. 'Welcome home!'

27

Brat noticed that her calm, determined face was also very pretty. Her hair was light in colour and fine as silk. 'Home,' he thought of her words, and felt happy.

'The trees are just beginning to flower. And the first foals are here. I hope you will think our horses are good. Aunt Bee says you're still interested in horses,' said Eleanor.

'Yes, but I haven't done much on the breeding side. Just preparing horses for work.'

They drove through the village of Clare and past the great gates at the entrance to Clare Park. A small boy was playing on one of the stone lions in front of the gates.

'Did you know Clare was a school nowadays?' said Eleanor.

Brat nearly said yes, but he remembered that this was one of the things Loding had told him, but not one that he was supposed to know.

'What kind of school?' he asked.

'A school for rich children who don't want to work. The children there are never forced to learn anything. The idea is that one day they will suddenly realize how important it is and want to learn. Of course, it doesn't work out like that.'

Brat smiled. 'What do they do all day, then?'

'I teach some of them to ride. They like that. It's not easy and most of the time they're so bored with easy things that they enjoy something more difficult – as long as it's something out of the ordinary. Ah, here we are, Latchetts.'

Brat felt his heart miss a beat as Eleanor turned slowly in through the white gateway. It was just as well that she was going slowly because suddenly a small figure in a blue dress rushed out from the trees and danced in front of the car. Eleanor stopped the car and shouted angrily at the dancing figure in blue, who paid no attention to her.

'Hullo! Hullo! Patrick! It's me! Ruth! I came to ride up with you. To the house. Can I sit on your knee? There isn't very much room in that little car of Eleanor's, and I don't want to get my dress dirty. I put it on specially for you coming home. Am I what you expected?'

She waited for an answer, so Brat said that he hadn't really thought about it.

'Oh,' said Ruth, disappointed. 'We've thought about you. No one has talked about anything else for days.'

'Ah well,' said Brat, 'when *you've* been away for years and years, people will talk about *you.*'

'I shouldn't dream of doing anything like that,' said Ruth, unforgiving.

As they drove towards Latchetts, Brat saw for the first time the surroundings which Alec Loding had painted for him in words. He waited for the moment when the house would appear, and for the moment when he would be face to face with his twin.

'Simon hasn't come back yet,' he heard Ruth say. From the way Ruth looked at Eleanor, Brat realized that something was not right and the family was worried about it. He reminded himself that other members of the family, especially Simon, might not accept him as easily as Bee had.

The car came out of the tree-lined drive and there stood Latchetts: a big old house. Brat's first thought was how friendly, quiet, and sure of itself the house looked. As the car stopped, he saw Bee coming down the steps. He had a sudden wish to tell her the truth and rush away without ever stepping into the house. He had no idea what to say to her.

It was Ruth who saved him. Before the car had completely stopped, she called out her own success, so that Brat's arrival somehow took second place.

'I met him after all, Aunt Bee! I met him after all! I came up from the gate with them. You don't mind, do you?'

She took hold of Brat's arm and pulled him out of the car. He

The car came out of the tree-lined drive and there stood Latchetts.

had become someone she had herself invited to Latchetts, and the difficult moment of meeting Bee again was over.

Before they had time to say anything, Jane came riding round the corner of the house on her pony, Fourposter, on the way to the stables. She tried to stop suddenly, and it was clear that she had not planned to be there when Brat arrived. But it was difficult to stop Fourposter when he was interested in something, and he came forward full of curiosity. Jane jumped down and unwillingly shook hands with Brat.

'What's your pony's name?' he asked, realising that she did not really want to welcome him.

'That's Fourposter,' said Ruth, before Jane had a chance to reply.

Brat put out his hand, but Fourposter looked away.

'He doesn't really like people,' said Jane, trying to apologize for her friend.

But Brat kept his hand out, and after a moment Fourposter changed his mind and dropped his head to Brat's waiting hand.

'Well!' said Ruth. 'He never does that for *anyone*!'

Brat looked down at the small, unsmiling face beside him.

'I expect he does for Jane, when no one is around,' he said.

'Jane,' said Bee. 'It's time to go and get washed before lunch.' She turned to lead the way indoors.

And Brat followed her through the front door and into Latchetts.

Chapter 7

Brat's first tests

'I've put you in the old nursery,' Bee said. 'I hope you don't mind. Simon has the room that he used to share with – that you used to share with him. And it didn't seem right to think of you as a visitor and give you one of the guest rooms.'

Brat said that he would be glad to have the nursery.

'Will you go up now,' said Bee, 'or will you have a drink first?'

'I'll go up now,' Brat said, and turned towards the stairs.

He knew that she had been waiting for this moment, the moment when he must show knowledge of the house. So he led the way upstairs, along the narrow passage to the children's rooms. He opened the third of the four doors and went into the room that Nora Ashby had arranged for her children when they were very small. He stood at the window, looking out at the green fields, and realized that there was something he had to say.

'Where's Simon?' he asked, and turned to Bee who had come into the room behind him.

'He's like Jane,' she replied. 'Late for lunch. But he'll be here soon. You'd better wash after your journey and come down at once. You can have the nursery bathroom all to yourself.'

She watched him as he went along the passage to the fourth door, which he knew was the bathroom door, and then she went downstairs feeling happier. He had known his way about the house. But Brat, on the other hand, was left feeling a little uneasy, even guilty. Cheating Mr Sandal had been like a game, and rather exciting, but cheating Bee Ashby was quite a different thing. It didn't seem right.

He washed and went back to his room where a young servant girl was looking for him. She stared at him with interest.

'Is there anything you need?' she asked.

'No, thank you,' said Brat.

'You're very like your brother, aren't you?' said the girl.

'I suppose so,' Brat replied.

'You won't know me, of course. I'm Lana Adams from the village. You look a lot older than your brother, don't you? I suppose because you've had a harder time than he has, out in the world, I mean. Having to look after yourself. Not spoilt like your brother. He's always had it too easy. That's why he's been so difficult about you coming back. Silly, I call it. You've only got to look at you to know you're an Ashby. Not much point in saying you're not, I should think. But you take my advice and stand up to him. He doesn't like that. Always gets everything too easily.'

As Brat went on quietly with his unpacking, Eleanor's cool voice came from the doorway:

'Have you everything you want?'

The girl said quickly, 'I was just welcoming Mr Patrick back,' and left the room.

'It's a nice room,' said Eleanor.

'Yes, the old wallpaper, I noticed,' said Brat, but he was busy thinking about what the village girl had said. So Simon refused to believe that he was Patrick. 'Not much point in saying you're not,' she had said. That could only mean that Simon refused to accept him.

Why?

He followed Eleanor downstairs into a big, sunny sitting room where Bee was pouring drinks. A few moments later the door opened and Simon Ashby came in.

He stopped for a moment, looking across at Brat.

'So you've come,' he said.

He walked slowly across the room until he was standing face to face with Brat by the window. There was no expression in his grey eyes, but Brat could feel the fear in Simon's body.

And then suddenly, the fear disappeared.

Simon stood for a moment searching Brat's face, and then his own face suddenly changed. His relief was obvious.

'They won't have told you,' he said, 'but I was prepared to deny, with my last breath, that you were Patrick. Now that I've seen you I take that all back. Of course you're Patrick.' He held out his hand.

'Welcome home.'

In the general happiness that followed Simon's words, Brat found himself grateful that the moment was over, but he was puzzled. What had Simon been afraid of? What had he been expecting? And why such obvious relief? It didn't seem to make sense.

He took the puzzle with him when they went in to lunch, and it lay in the back of his mind as they ate and talked, mostly

'*Welcome home.*'

about horses. He noticed that Ruth was the only member of the family who called him Patrick, and Brat began to wish that Jane would be more friendly towards him. If he had ever had a younger sister, he would have liked her to be just like Jane.

One thing helped him greatly in this first difficult meeting with the Ashbys. The story he had to tell was true, except for the beginning. It was the story of his own life. And the family was very careful not to talk about the beginnings, the running away that had led him into that life.

After dinner Bee offered Brat a cigarette, but he preferred a different kind and took out his own cigarette-case to offer it round. Bee refused, but Eleanor took the case and carefully read the name inside.

'Brat Farrar,' she said. 'Who's that?'

'Me,' said Brat.

'You? Oh yes, Farrar, of course. But why Brat?'

'I don't know. I suppose they called me that because I was small.'

'Brat!' Ruth was delighted. 'Do you mind if I call you Brat?'

'No. It's been my name for a large part of my life.'

The door opened and Lana appeared to say that a young man from one of the newspapers had called to see Miss Ashby.

'Oh, not already,' said Bee. 'Which newspaper? Did he say why he had come?'

'It's the local paper, the *Westover Times*. He says he's come about Mr Patrick,' said Lana.

'Come on, Brat,' said Bee. 'We'd better see him. You too, Simon.' She took Brat by the hand and led him out of the dining room, still laughing about his name. The warmth and friendliness of her hand sent a strange feeling through Brat's heart. It was like nothing he had so far experienced in life, but he liked it.

A young man in a blue suit was waiting for them in the hall. 'Miss Ashby? My name's Macallan, from the *Westover Times*.

I don't want to take up much of your time.'

'I suppose you want to know about my nephew's coming home,' said Bee.

'Just that,' replied the young man. 'Which of these young men has just come back from the dead?'

Bee introduced Brat and Simon and they all answered the questions Mr Macallan asked.

'Why is the *Westover Times* interested?' asked Bee. 'When my nephew disappeared eight years ago, there was hardly anything in the paper about it. This is of no possible interest to anyone, except his family.'

'You're wrong there, Miss Ashby,' said the newspaper reporter. 'People disappear every day, people die every day, and the newspapers aren't very interested. But the number of people who come back from the dead, like your nephew, is very small.'

Chapter 8

Battle begins

After Mr Macallan had gone, Bee suggested that they should all go and look at the horses. Brat did not have any proper riding clothes, so Simon said, 'Come up with me, and I'll find you something to wear.'

Brat followed Simon upstairs and into the room that Simon had once shared with his brother. He noticed at once that it was very much Simon's own room; there was no suggestion that he had ever shared it with another person. It was as much a sitting room as a bedroom, with shelves of books and silver cups which Simon had won in riding competitions.

Simon brought a jacket and a pair of trousers out of a cupboard and saw Brat looking at a small silver cup. He smiled and said, 'I took that from you, if you remember. It was my first cup.'

'From me?' said Brat, unprepared.

'Yes. You would have won on Old Harry, but I jumped a perfect second round on my horse.'

'Oh yes,' Brat said, and looked at all the other cups. 'You seem to have done well for yourself since then.'

'Not badly,' said Simon. 'But I'm going to do a lot better. By the way, do you remember the thing that used to hang at the end of your bed?' he asked casually.

'The little wooden horse?' Brat said. 'Yes, of course. Travesty,' he added, giving its name. 'There was a joke about its imaginary parents, wasn't there? Bog Oak and Irish Peasant.'

Brat looked round and in the mirror he saw the sudden, terrible shock in Simon's face. But Simon recovered quickly and turned round with a shirt in his hand.

'Here you are. I think you'll find that fits all right.'

Brat took the shirt and went off to his own room, feeling rather shocked himself. What did it mean? Ashby hadn't expected him to know that. Ashby had been certain that he would not know about the toy horse called Travesty, and he had been surprised, no, totally shocked, when it was clear that Brat did know about it.

That could mean only one thing.

It meant that Simon had not believed for a moment that he was the real Patrick. But why bother to pretend? Why hadn't he said at once, 'You're not Patrick, and nothing will make me believe that you are!'

From what Lana had said, Simon had intended to say just that. So why had he changed his mind? Was it a trap? Did Simon's friendly welcome simply hide some trap that he had prepared?

But Simon could not have known until they met that he, Brat, was not the real Patrick. And when they did meet, he seemed to have known immediately that the person in front of him was not his real brother. Why then should he accept Brat as Patrick?

As Brat got dressed in the borrowed riding clothes, he thought hard about these questions and then he stopped. He had remembered something. He had remembered the fear in Simon's face when they first met, and then the sudden change of fear into relief.

That was it! Simon had been afraid that he *was* Patrick.

When he realised that he was faced with an imposter, he was relieved. But if he was so sure that Brat was an imposter, why was he willing to recognize Brat as his brother? Was Simon just waiting for Brat to make some mistake which would prove that he was not Patrick? Perhaps Simon was playing a cruel game, like boys who liked pulling wings off flies.

'If that's your plan, young Mr Ashby, you're going to have a few surprises,' Brat thought to himself. Simon had not yet learnt that Brat had passed the first difficult 'family' tests, and he had probably been looking forward to preparing several other unpleasant traps for the imposter.

Travesty had been the first. The little wooden horse was something that only Patrick or someone in the family would know about. Who else could possibly know about Patrick's favourite toy when he was a child?

And Brat had known about it. It was not surprising, therefore, that Simon had been so shocked and confused.

Brat thought gratefully about his excellent teacher, Alec Loding. Loding had missed his profession; he might be a bad actor, but he was a wonderful teacher. The time spent in Kew Gardens learning about the Ashby family had been time well spent.

As he finished dressing, Brat felt a new sense of excitement which replaced the guilt he had felt with Bee and the children.

The dangerous game had become a battle, and Simon was his enemy.

He went downstairs where the rest of the family were waiting for him.

'Come on,' said Bee. 'Let's go and look at the stables first.' She put one arm through Brat's and took Simon's with her other arm, so that they went off to the stables like three old friends. Eleanor and the twins followed along behind.

Brat enjoyed the walk around the stables. At first he was amused. The place looked too pretty to be real. There were flowers in pots and the buildings were clean and brightly painted. There was no sign of any mud or dirt. Brat began to tell himself that the horses must have a very soft and easy life – unlike the hard-working horses he had been used to in the States. His opinion changed after he had seen a few horses in their boxes. These were not just pretty pets. Their shining coats were the result of hard work and careful attention, not of soft and easy living.

By the time they came to the last three boxes Simon and Brat were alone.

'These last ones are all horses we've bought recently,' said Simon. 'They're all good, but this is the best one of them all. He's a four-year-old called Timber.'

Timber was completely black, except for a white star on his head. Brat thought he was the most handsome horse he had ever seen. But there was something else about him. Simon brought Timber out of his box and the horse stood there, pleased to be admired, but carefully watching his admirers.

'Difficult to find anything wrong with him, isn't it?' said Simon.

'He's a beautiful horse,' said Brat, 'but doesn't he look pleased with himself?'

'Well, I suppose he's got good reason to be pleased. He's a

lovely horse to ride, too, and he can jump over anything.'

Brat moved forward to the horse and put his hand up to touch its head. Timber looked rather bored.

'He hasn't had any exercise yet today,' said Simon. 'Would you like to take him out?'

'I certainly would.'

Simon called a stableman over. 'Arthur, bring a saddle for Timber.'

'Yes sir.'

While Timber was being saddled, they looked at the other two new horses.

'What are you going to ride?' asked Brat.

Simon turned to face him. 'I thought you would like to have a look round by yourself. But don't let him get too hot.'

'No, I'll bring him back cool,' said Brat, putting his leg over his first English horse. As he turned the horse towards the gate at the end of the stables, Simon said, 'He has his tricks, so be careful.'

Brat rode Timber gently to the first gate, opened it, went through and turned to close it behind him. Timber knew all about gates and behaved perfectly. They went on to the soft grassland of the hills, and at a sign from Brat, Timber began to canter up the hill. Brat remembered how wonderful it was to ride a horse that did everything its rider wanted; but with Timber it was better than he had ever known before. Along the top of the hill was a wide, level grass path and Timber flew along. It seemed that his feet were hardly touching the ground.

Brat had ridden fast horses before, but never one that moved as smoothly as Timber. The soft, sweet air sailed past his face and he heard the sound of Timber's galloping feet. 'Who cares, who cares, who cares!' said the sound, and Brat felt that even if he died tomorrow, it didn't matter. They came to the end of the path and Timber stopped, giving Brat a chance to look at the countryside below them. He could see the roofs of Latchetts and the stables, and a little further away was the village of Clare with its church. Brat remembered the map he had looked at so often with Alec Loding and began to recognize what before he had seen only on paper. He looked down on a hill called Tanbitches, but there were now only seven beech trees instead of ten. On the other side of Tanbitches was a path that led to the coast, the path where Patrick Ashby had last been seen on that day eight years ago.

It was suddenly more real to Brat than it had ever been before; the terrible death of Patrick Ashby, this death which he was now using to his own advantage.

Brat looked across at the path along which a boy had gone, so loaded with misery that the beautiful green English surroundings had meant nothing to him. He had had horses like Timber, a loving family, friends, a home, and it had all meant nothing to him.

Brat felt very sorry for Patrick Ashby.

Chapter 9

He has his tricks

Brat slid from Timber's back and sat down on the grass to take a longer look at the green English countryside. Timber stood quietly eating the soft grass, and Brat sat, half in a dream.

He was woken by a girl's voice behind him:

'Don't look,

Don't move,

Shut your eyes,

And guess who.'

Naturally Brat disobeyed the instructions and looked round

to see the face of a girl of about sixteen. When her eyes met Brat's they grew wide with sudden alarm.

'Oh!' she cried. 'I thought you were Simon. You're not.'

'No,' agreed Brat, beginning to get to his feet.

But before he could move, she had dropped to the grass beside him.

'My, you gave me a shock. But I know who you are. You're the long-lost brother, aren't you? You must be; you're so like Simon. You even wear the same kind of clothes. I'm Sheila Parslow. I'm at the school at Clare Park.'

'Oh,' said Brat, remembering what Eleanor had said – a school for rich children where the pupils didn't have to do any work.

'I'm doing my best to make Simon fall in love with me, but it's difficult,' said Sheila Parslow. 'He often comes riding up here because he hates Tanbitches. That's the hill over there. He never goes there. And when I saw that big black horse, I was sure it was him. I've got to do something to make life at Clare Park more exciting. It's so boring. We're allowed to do anything we like, just anything.'

'Does Simon know you're fond of him?'

'Fond of him? I don't think I like him at all. I'm just looking for something exciting to do. But Simon is only interested in the Gates girl. Do you know her?' asked Sheila Parslow. 'I'm even taking riding lessons, but that doesn't seem to help.'

'Well, I don't see that I can help you very much, either,' said Brat. 'And I'm afraid I've got to go,' he went on, as he got up from the grass.

'I wish you didn't have to go. You're the nicest person I've met since I came to Clare. Simon told me your name, of course, but I forget. What is it?'

'Patrick.'

As he said the name, his mind went back to Patrick going

along that path on the other side of the valley, from Tanbitches to the coast, and he forgot Miss Parslow immediately.

Brat rode Timber slowly back along the path and then downhill towards Latchetts. At the bottom he could see that the gate had been left open and he pressed Timber into a canter.

It was Brat's years of experience of rough riding that saved him. Just before the gate Timber turned suddenly to the right, brushing his left side hard against the fence. Brat's leg should have been crushed between the saddle and the fence. But Brat had moved as quickly as lightning and had pulled his leg out of the way.

Brat pulled Timber to a stop.

'Well, you *have* got your own little tricks, haven't you?' he accused, as Timber stood quietly in the centre of the path, ears up, listening to Brat's voice. 'I know men who'd give you a real beating for trying a trick like that,' he said as he turned Timber back to approach the open gate again. This time, as Brat had expected, Timber cantered straight through the gate without looking to either side and continued straight towards Latchetts. For Timber nothing wrong had ever happened.

At the entrance to the stables he met Eleanor.

'Hullo!' she said. 'Have you been out on Timber?' She sounded a little surprised. 'I hope Simon warned you about him.'

'Yes, thank you. He told me about his tricks.'

'One of my bad buys,' she said, looking at Timber.

'Yours?' he said.

'Yes. I bought him at the Lerridge Sale. It was Timber who killed old Felix, the Master of the Hunt, but I thought that had been an accident. No one told me that Timber had tried to do exactly the same thing to another rider a few days later. That's why I got him quite cheap, because he's so dangerous.'

'He's certainly a very good-looking horse,' said Brat.

Timber turned suddenly to the right.

'He's beautiful,' Eleanor said. 'And a wonderful jumper. But he's very dangerous. Did he try any tricks today?'

'Just a little one at the gate,' replied Brat.

'Most of the time he behaves perfectly. That's why he's so dangerous when he plays one of his tricks. It's always when you don't expect it.'

'He's certainly got a very high opinion of himself,' said Brat. 'I don't think I've ever seen a horse looking so self-confident.'

'Well, I expect I'd have a good opinion of myself if I were a horse who was clever enough to kill a man and make it seem like an accident.'

Brat, thinking it over, agreed with her. Timber was unusual: an intelligent but deliberately dangerous horse.

And Brat thought also about Simon, who had sent him out on a killer horse with no more than a light remark about the horse 'having its tricks'.

That evening Bee Ashby looked down the dining-table at her nephew Patrick and thought how well he was managing. It was a difficult situation for him. George and Nancy Peck had joined them for dinner, but Brat was quiet and relaxed with a calm self-confidence.

Bee had brought Simon up, and she was pleased with the result. But this boy had brought himself up, and the result was even better, she thought. Patrick had always seemed to have much goodness in him, and the result was this quiet, adult young man with the still face.

Simon was being particularly cheerful and Bee felt very sorry for him. He had accepted that Latchetts was no longer his, and he was being sensible about it. Bee had not believed that the selfish, money-conscious Simon would behave so well.

Brat, too, at the other end of the table, was watching Simon, but did not feel sorry for him. It was not because Simon was his enemy; he had admired enemies before now. It was because there was something about Simon Ashby that he disliked very strongly. Simon sat there being very cheerful so that everyone felt sorry for him. Only Brat knew that this was all an act, that Simon was only pretending to accept the return of his older brother so easily.

Watching Simon's charm and his good manners, Brat felt that Simon reminded him of someone he had met recently. Who could that be? Not Alec Loding, not Mr Sandal. No. Then who could it be?

Later that night, as Brat lay in his bed in the old nursery at Latchetts, he thought about the events of that first day. He thought about Bee Ashby – how kindly she had helped him through the difficult moments, how happily she had accepted him at Latchetts, how she had given him the feeling that he belonged there. That was a feeling he had never known before, being part of a family.

He went on thinking of Bee as he fell asleep. She was a lovely, kind woman and he loved her for her warm friendliness.

Brat was just falling asleep when he remembered something and was suddenly awake again. He knew who it was that Simon Ashby reminded him of.

It was Timber.

Chapter 10

Patrick's death

On Wednesday morning Bee took Brat to call on the farmers who rented the three farms on the Latchetts estate. The last and smallest one was Wigsell, where the Gates family lived and worked. Mr Gates had another larger farm not far away, and also a butcher's shop, and so was not short of money. He spent most of it on his daughter, Peggy, whom he loved very much.

'They tell me you've been making money in horses in America, Mr Patrick,' he said to Brat.

'I've earned my living from them.'

'Well, come and see what I've got in *my* stable.' He led them round to the back of the house. 'Now then, have you ever seen such a fine horse as this?'

One of the stablemen led out a beautiful brown horse which Bee recognized at once.

'Isn't that Dick Pope's horse, the one that won all the cups at the Bath and West Show last year?' she cried.

'That's right,' said Mr Gates proudly. 'Cost me a lot of money, but nothing's too good for my girl Peggy.'

'You've certainly got a good horse, Mr Gates. Peggy's a very lucky girl. Is she going to jump it in shows this year?' asked Bee.

'Of course she is, of course she is! That's what I bought it for.'

Brat was puzzled by how pleased Bee sounded. After all, if this brown horse was so good, it would be competing against Timber and the other Latchetts horses, and perhaps beating them. On the way home Bee still looked so pleased that Brat said to her, 'You look like a cat that's just been given a saucer of milk.'

'Milk *and* fish,' she said, amused, but did not tell him what

47

she meant.

Before lunch Bee told Eleanor about the visits to the farms.

'Do you remember that brown horse that won everything at the Bath Show last year?'

'Dick Pope's horse? Certainly.'

'Gates has bought it for Peggy to show.'

'Well, well!' said Eleanor slowly; and she looked amused and pleased. Her eyes met Bee's and she said: 'I don't know that that was such a very good idea.'

'No, I think you may be right,' answered Bee.

The twins came in from school and Simon from the stables, and together they went in for lunch.

Simon seemed interested to hear about Brat's visits to the farms and Bee told him everything that had happened. When she got to Wigsell, Eleanor said:

'Did you know that Gates has bought Peggy a new horse?'

'No,' said Simon, looking up with interest.

'He's bought her that brown horse of Dick Pope's.'

'Riding Light?'

'Yes. Riding Light. She's going to show it this year.'

For the first time since he had met him Brat saw Simon's face go red with anger. Simon said nothing, and after a moment went on with his lunch. Neither Bee nor Eleanor looked at him.

And Brat thought hard. Simon Ashby was supposed to be crazy about the Gates girl. But was he glad that she had been given a good horse? No. He was angry. He couldn't bear the idea that she had a horse good enough to beat him. Brat remembered how pleased Bee had been with the brown horse. He saw again Eleanor's slow amusement at the news. The two women had known at once that that would be the end of Simon's interest in Peggy. Gates had bought Riding Light so that his daughter would have a really good horse. A horse as good as any of Simon's horses. He hoped that Peggy would marry Simon, but in fact he had destroyed her chances of ever marrying him. What kind of creature was this Simon Ashby, who hated the thought that he could be beaten by the girl he was in love with?

When he went to bed that night, Brat was still puzzling over the problem of Simon. Simon, who was quite sure that Brat was not the real Patrick, but who did not intend to say so. Why not? Simon, who was so good at pretending that even his family did not know his deepest feelings. Simon, who was so self-centred, so selfish. Simon, who was like Timber.

If Simon felt so strongly about Peggy Gates owning a better horse, he must also, Brat thought, have very strong feelings about Patrick's sudden return. He thought about this for a long time, staring into the dark, and another question came. 'I wonder where Simon was when Patrick fell over that cliff?'

But he realised at once that this was nonsense. The police had carefully investigated Patrick's death. They must have asked Simon where he was that day. Still, Brat felt curious. He would go and read about it in the local newspaper, just to be sure of what had happened.

The next day Bee wanted to go shopping in Westover and Brat went with her to visit the town. He went to the offices of the *Westover Times*, where Mr Macallan helped him to find the old copy of the newspaper which had reported the death of Patrick Ashby eight years before. Brat sat down to read about 'his' death.

Saturday afternoon had been a holiday for the Ashby children. Simon had mechanical interests and Patrick's hobby was bird-watching. No one had worried about him until after dinner as everybody thought he was just late. When he failed to appear after dark everyone – family, friends and police – set out to look for him, but without success. Next morning Patrick's jacket was found at the top of the cliffs, just where the path from Tanbitches led down to the harbour at Westover. There was a note in the pocket of the jacket. If Patrick had fallen into the sea below the cliffs, his body would not be found near Westover as the sea would carry it much further west.

The last person to see Patrick Ashby was a farm-worker called Abel Tusk. He had met Patrick in the early afternoon, about half-way between Tanbitches and the cliff. Patrick was lying in the grass watching for birds, and seemed to be the same quiet, serious boy that he usually was.

Bee had told the police that the death of his parents had been a very great shock to Patrick, but that he had taken it well and seemed to be recovering. She had no reason to think that he would take his own life. She was asked if she recognized the writing on the note found in Patrick's jacket.

'Oh, yes. Patrick had a very special way of writing his capital letters. And he was the only person I know who used a stylograph.'

She explained that a stylograph was a special kind of pen that Patrick owned. It was black and had thin yellow lines round it. And it had not been found, although he always carried it with him.

The police decided that the only explanation for Patrick's death was that, in a sudden desperate moment, he had thrown himself over the cliff. His home was now empty of the happiness he had shared with his parents. Perhaps the thought of going back to it had been too much for him. And that was the death of Patrick Ashby according to the *Westover Times*.

Brat sat back in the quiet newspaper office and thought about it all. The boy lying in the grass watching birds. And night coming. And no boy coming home across Tanbitches hill.

And nothing in the newspaper about where Simon had been that afternoon.

When he joined Bee for lunch, he told her how he had spent his morning.

'How horrible!' she said at first. Then, 'No, of course it isn't. It's what we would all like to be able to do, to read the report of our own death. Did you find it interesting?'

'Yes. I can't remember, Bee, what Simon's mechanical interests were at that time.'

'Mechanical interests? I don't think Simon ever had any. Why do you ask?'

'Well, that's what you told the police, to explain why Simon and I didn't do things together. And I can't remember what Simon used to do either,' said Brat, casually.

'It's stupid of me, Brat, but I have no idea. I don't even remember where Simon was that day. I do remember that he spent all night out on his pony looking for you. I don't know if you realize it, Brat, but what you did was very difficult for Simon. He changed after you went. He was a different person afterwards.'

Since Brat had no answer to this, he ate in silence. After a moment Bee went on: 'And you made life very difficult for me, too, by never writing to me. Why didn't you ever write, Brat?'

This was the weak point in Brat's whole story, as Loding had frequently told him.

'I don't *know*,' Brat said. 'Honestly, I don't know!'

'All right,' she said, 'I won't worry you, my dear. I didn't mean to. It's just something that has puzzled me. I was very fond of you, and we were such very good friends. It was not like you to live a life of your own without once looking back.'

'It's easier than you think to drop the past behind you when you're thirteen. You're always meeting new experiences, I mean, and you just go on.'

'I must try running away one day,' she said lightly. 'There's a lot of the past I should like to drop behind me.'

Chapter 11

Patrick's birthday

Brat had not thought about Patrick's twenty-first birthday at all. It had been decided not to celebrate the birthday officially until after Bee's Uncle Charles returned to England. But Brat had forgotten that there would still be a day on which he, as Patrick, would be twenty-one. When he came down to breakfast that Friday morning, he was surprised to find a pile of parcels on the table beside his plate. There was, of course, another pile of presents beside Simon's plate.

'Happy birthday, Brat!' they said as they came in. 'Happy birthday, Brat!' One after another.

He wished he didn't feel so bad about it. He wished that they were really his family and that it really was his birthday. It was a very nice thing, a family birthday.

Mr Sandal had come down to Latchetts the previous day and after breakfast he took Brat into the quiet library of the house. 'Patrick' had to sign a lot of papers to mark his coming-of-age and taking over responsibility for Latchetts and his mother's fortune. Brat listened carefully as Mr Sandal explained how the estate had been managed over the last eight years, some good years, some bad years. On the whole the estate had paid its way, thanks to Bee's careful management.

Brat discovered that the monthly allowances paid to Simon and Eleanor were rather small and suggested that they should be increased. Mr Sandal agreed; he thought that Simon would probably go somewhere else to start his own business and would need help from the estate to do this.

Brat thought to himself that Simon was more likely to stay at Latchetts, waiting for his chance, like Timber.

That afternoon Brat decided to walk by himself over Tanbitches hill by the path that Patrick had taken on the last day of his life. As he came near the top and the young trees round the old quarry, he found an old man sitting on the grass watching his sheep. He greeted the old man politely and was on his way past when the man spoke;

'A bit proud, aren't you?'

Brat turned and looked at the old man.

'Not many nests you'd ever have seen, but for me,' went on the old man.

'Abel! Abel Tusk!' said Brat, remembering the report he had read about Patrick's death. 'Am I glad to see you!' Brat sat down on the grass beside the old man. Abel had been the last person to see Patrick alive, but Brat learned nothing more from him to explain why Patrick had killed himself. Abel had been just as shocked as everyone else. And now he was delighted that he had been right – he had never believed that Patrick had killed himself.

On his way down the hill Brat heard the sound of hammer on metal and came to the workshop where the blacksmith was making horseshoes. The smith, Mr Pilbeam, stopped work to welcome him, but had to continue at once while the iron was still hot. Brat helped him to heat up the fire, saying, 'I've earned my living at this since you saw me last.'

'You have, Mr Patrick? I don't believe it. Here!' and he held out a half-made shoe. 'Would you like to finish this one off?' Brat accepted the challenge with a smile and made a good job of it. Mr Pilbeam looked on and was well satisfied with the result.

'Funny,' he said, 'if any Ashby was going to earn his living at

'Would you like to finish this one off?'

54

this job, it ought to have been your brother.'

'Why?'

'There was a time when he was always in here, planning to make things. He never made very much, but for months he was always around the place. He was in here helping me the day you ran away. I had to chase him home for his supper. But you, you never took much interest in this kind of work when you were a boy.'

As Brat walked back towards Latchetts he thought about this answer to the question that had been worrying him. He knew now where Simon had been that afternoon, nowhere near the cliffs where Patrick had last been seen.

Near the house he met Jane. He thought she had been waiting for him and she greeted him shyly.

'I wanted to say something to you. Do you mind?' she said very seriously.

'Something you want me to do for you, Jane?' he asked.

'Oh no, nothing like that. It's just that I wasn't very nice to you when you came home from America, and I want to apologize.'

'Oh Jane,' said Brat, wanting to hold the small brave girl in his arms. 'What you felt was a very natural thing to feel. I understand now, and I did then, too.'

'Then you'll accept my apology?'

'I accept your apology,' said Brat quietly. They shook hands and walked back to the house in friendly silence.

In the following days Brat settled down to life at Latchetts. He worked with the horses, helping to train them and keep them in good condition, and spent a great deal of time learning from Eleanor all about the work of Latchetts stud.

Bee watched Eleanor and Brat becoming close friends with pleasure, but she wished that Simon had more share in it. Simon seemed to find more and more reasons for being away from

Latchetts, and Bee suspected that he was drinking more than was good for him. Perhaps he was still finding it difficult to accept the new situation, thought Bee, but she hoped that he would soon become one of the team that Eleanor and Brat were making.

'You'll have to do *something* at the Bures Show,' said Eleanor one day, as they came in tired from the stables. 'It's the biggest show in the local year. People will think it very strange if you don't do anything at all.'

Brat had already said that he would not try to 'show' any horses at Bures. 'Perhaps I could ride in one of the races at the end.'

'But they're just for fun. That isn't the serious work with horses,' said Eleanor. 'Still, it would be better than doing nothing.'

They talked about it with Bee, who was happy to agree that Brat would ride one of her horses, Chevron.

Bee had been delighted to find that Brat had a real interest in horses, much more than Simon had. Simon only knew as much about horse breeding as was necessary for his work. Brat found great pleasure in studying all the books about breeding in the Latchetts library and spent hours discussing the subject with Bee and Eleanor.

Bee was well pleased not only at her nephew's return, but also at the kind of person who had returned. She thought about all the shapes that Patrick could have appeared in, and found that Brat was just what she would have wanted.

Because it was Simon who would show Timber and jump him at the Bures Show, Brat left Timber's training completely to Simon and worked only with the other horses. But there were days when Simon was away from Latchetts and someone had to take Timber out. Brat looked forward to those days. Timber was challenge, and excitement, and satisfaction. Brat planned to stop Timber brushing people off his back, but not yet, not until after the Bures Show. As he rode around the countryside he looked for a good place for this lesson, but could find none on Latchetts land. He thought of Clare Park and one day asked Eleanor:

'Do the people at the school mind if we ride through Clare Park?'

'No, as long as we keep away from the playing fields.'

So Brat took Timber to the other side of the valley and cantered him gently around the soft grass, looking carefully at the height of the lowest branches of the large trees. Timber followed all of this with puzzled interest. He knew why *he* liked large trees with low branches, but why did this man find the same trees so interesting?

'Are you looking for me?' said a voice once day, and Sheila Parslow appeared from behind a large tree.

Brat apologized and said that he was looking for a place to teach Timber good manners.

'What's the matter with his manners?' said the girl.

'He likes to turn suddenly under a tree so that he brushes his rider off his back. He killed a man like that.'

Miss Parslow looked at Timber with new interest.

'You don't say. I never thought these stupid animals had that much sense. How are you going to stop him?'

'I'm going to make riding under trees a painful experience for him,' said Brat.

'And will that change him?'

'I hope so. Next time he sees a suitable tree, he'll remember how much it hurt the last time he tried to brush his rider off.'

Brat realized that he hadn't seen Sheila around the stables in the last few days. He asked her how her riding was getting on.

'I've given it up. If I want to see Simon I know where I can find him.'

'Oh, where's that?' said Brat before he could stop himself.

'In the bar at the Angel pub in Westover,' she replied. 'He's beginning to get quite friendly. He's not at all interested in the Gates girl now.'

Brat thought about this as he walked Timber home. He knew that Sheila Parslow's father was very, very rich, and that Simon now needed money. But surely Simon wouldn't think of marrying Sheila Parslow just for her money? Simon was a difficult person to understand.

In the stables Eleanor had found the Latchett racing shirts, in the colours that Brat would have to wear at the Bures races.

'I expect they'll fit you all right, but we'll take them up to the house and see, shall we? Now we'd better go, or we'll be late for dinner,' she said.

Together they walked out of the stables and came face to face with Simon.

'Oh, you're back, Simon,' Eleanor was beginning, when she caught sight of his face.

'Who had Timber out?' he said, white with anger.

'I did,' said Brat.

'Timber is *my* business and you have no right to take him out.'

'Someone had to take him out today,' Brat said quietly.

'*No one* takes Timber out but me. *No one.*'

'But Simon,' said Eleanor, 'the horses are Brat's, and if anyone says who does what, it must be him.'

'Shut up!' shouted Simon. 'I won't have some clumsy fool harming a good horse like Timber.'

'*Simon! Really!* You must be drunk to talk like that about your own brother,' cried Eleanor.

'My brother! *That!* Why, you poor little fool, he isn't even an Ashby. God knows who he is. Some stupid stableman. That's what he should be doing, cleaning out the stables. After this,' he

58

'My brother! That!'

59

turned to Brat, 'you leave alone the horses that I intend to ride.'

Simon's face was very close to Brat's. Brat could easily have knocked Simon down, and he remembered the fights he had fought in his time in America. But this time Eleanor was there, and he would never do anything like that in front of her.

'Well, did you hear me?' shouted Simon, angered by Brat's silence.

'I heard you,' Brat said.

'Well, remember what I said. Timber is *my* business.' And he walked quickly off towards the house.

Eleanor looked shocked and worried.

'Oh Brat, I'm sorry. I'm so sorry. He had that mad idea that you weren't Patrick before he ever saw you. He's obviously been drinking and I suppose the thought came from the back of his mind and he said it because he was angry. When he's angry, he always says things he doesn't mean.'

It was Brat's experience that when people were very angry, or drunk, they often said exactly what they really thought. But he didn't tell Eleanor that. He just said that everyone made a fool of themselves sometime or other when they had drunk too much, and she shouldn't bother about it.

Simon did not come in to dinner that evening, but when he came in to breakfast the following morning he was his usual sunny self.

'I'm afraid I was drunk last night. And very rude. I apologize.' And he looked innocently at Eleanor and Brat, the only other people at the table.

'You were quite horrible,' Eleanor said coldly.

But the air cleared, and the day was just another day. The Ashby family settled back into its preparations for that day at Bures that was going to change all their lives.

Chapter 12

The Bures show

Bures was a small town not far north of Westover. The Show, for horses and other farm animals, which happened every year was very much like the same kind of show that happened in most English country towns. Bures was in the middle of rich farming land and its Show was, therefore, more important than most. The Show was not just for showing the best farm animals and doing business, it was also a time when the best-known families for miles around came together. The day always ended with a 'Dance' for everyone who wanted people to think that they were very fashionable.

The Ashbys always rented the same bedrooms in the Chequers Hotel and they all went over by car on Wednesday morning.

'It's going to be perfect weather,' said Eleanor looking at the cloudless sky. 'Somehow it nearly always is at Bures. What are you going to do for the morning, Brat?'

'I'm going to walk round the race-course, just to see what I've got to do in the race.'

'How right you are. Just as sensible as ever, Brat.'

'Well, everybody else probably knows it much better than I do,' said Brat.

'Don't you ever get excited, Brat, with your stomach turning over?' asked Eleanor.

'Yes, over and over,' he replied.

'That's interesting. With you it doesn't show. With me, as you can see, my face goes a dull kind of pink. Yours is a very useful kind of face to have.'

Brat thought that the warm pink of Eleanor's face was lovely, but didn't dare say so.

'Have you ever seen Peggy Gates on a horse?' Eleanor said. 'She rides very well and she looks very nice.'

Brat walked round the race-course, and was happy to find that there were no unexpected surprises or hidden problems. He went back to join the rest of the family for lunch and afterwards found himself alone with Ruth.

Ruth did not like riding, and was bored by horses. But she desperately wanted her twin sister Jane to do well, and was probably just as excited as Jane herself.

'That's Roger Clint with Eleanor,' she told Brat.

'Where?' Brat saw Eleanor talking to a tall, dark-haired, handsome young man. 'Who's Roger Clint?'

'He's got a big farm near here,' replied Ruth. 'He's in love with Eleanor.'

'A very good person to be in love with,' Brat said, but his heart felt heavy.

The first part of the Show went very well. Jane, wearing her best riding-clothes, took her horse Rajah round the course without a mistake and won the class for young riders of her age. Ruth was delighted, as were the rest of the Ashby family.

Later came the most important event of the day, the Open Jumping Prize. After the first round only Eleanor, Simon, Peggy Gates and Roger Clint had done well enough to go on to the second round. Simon had ridden Timber beautifully and Timber seemed pleased with himself. Peggy Gates on Riding Light also had a perfect first round, but on the second her horse knocked one fence down.

When Simon came out for the second round, he looked very white and clearly determined to beat the girl who had just completed a nearly perfect round. But Timber looked puzzled.

'I've done this once,' he seemed to say. 'Why have I got to do it again?' But he jumped well and Simon concentrated hard on making sure that the horse made no mistakes. Suddenly Simon's hat blew off in the wind and a small dog rushed out to chase it. Timber turned sharply away, frightened, and the crowd went very quiet. Patiently and quietly Simon talked to his horse until Timber was calm again and jumped the last fence beautifully.

Simon had won.

The afternoon went on, and then Brat decided to get ready for the race which would come at the end of the day. Every time he had seen Eleanor she seemed to be with Roger Clint and enjoying his company, and Brat felt miserable.

'What's it got to do with you?' said a voice inside him. 'You're her brother, remember.'

'Shut up!' he told the voice unhappily.

Chevron, the horse that Brat was going to ride in the race, was upset and worried by the noise of the crowd and Brat took her for a walk in the park. When he came back, he met Simon who said it was time to go down to the start.

'Did you remember to sign the book?' Simon asked.

'Book?' said Brat. 'Sign for what?'

'To show that you agree to your horse running in the race. Everybody's got to do it.'

'All right. Where's the book?'

'Down at the office. I'll look after Chevron for you till you come back. Don't worry, I'll keep her calm.'

Brat went down and signed the book.

'Well, Mr Ashby, your family has been doing very well today. Three firsts. Are you going to make it a fourth?'

When Brat returned to Chevron, he found one of the stablemen looking after her.

'Mr Simon said he couldn't wait, Mr Patrick, but he said to wish you luck. He's gone to watch with the rest of the family. Good luck, sir.'

Brat was just about to get on Chevron when he thought that

he ought to check the saddle belt once more. He had already fixed it once, but perhaps he had made it too tight.

But when he looked, he found that someone had loosened it. Just a little, but enough to make sure that the saddle would slip dangerously about half-way round the race. Another of Simon's tricks!

Brat fixed the saddle belt and went down to the start. As he arrived, he met Roger Clint.

'You're Patrick Ashby, aren't you?' he said. 'My name's Roger Clint.' They shook hands. 'It's nice to have you at Bures again.'

'Who won the last race?' asked Brat.

'I did. Eleanor was very close behind. But she won it last year, so it's time someone else won it. And I wanted a silver cup, anyway.'

Brat had no time to ask why Roger wanted a silver cup so much. It was time to start the last race.

Brat had a careful look at the other horses. Most of them had been ridden so much already that day that they would probably be too tired for a long race. But there were three other good horses that he would have to watch.

At the start of the race Brat was happy to let some of the others go first. Chevron liked seeing other horses in front of her and seemed to be enjoying herself. She jumped smoothly and confidently. Brat watched as other horses fell or became tired, and Chevron began to move towards the front. Roger Clint's horse, Stockings, seemed the best of the others, the one that he would have to beat, so he moved up beside it. Clint gave him a friendly smile, but he was having to push his horse hard. Brat decided that Stockings was getting very tired. About four hundred metres from the finish, he decided to try to trick Clint out of the race. Chevron was running side by side with Stockings, but Brat pulled her back a little so that Stockings

Brat pushed Chevron to go as fast as possible towards the finish.

went a little in front. Clint thought that this meant that Chevron had become too tired. He relaxed a little, and at that moment Brat pushed Chevron to go as fast as possible towards the finish. Before Clint realized what had happened, Chevron had passed Stockings and Brat had stolen the race.

'What a fool I am to fall for such an old trick,' laughed Roger Clint as he and Brat walked their horses back after the race.

And Brat felt that he liked Roger Clint quite a lot, even if Eleanor was going to marry him.

65

Chapter 13

Simon confesses

'I've never seen Simon so pleased with himself,' Eleanor said, watching Simon over Brat's shoulder as they danced together that night. 'Usually when he wins he doesn't bother making much of it.'

Brat said it was probably the champagne, and turned her away from her view of Simon.

He had looked forward all day to dancing with Eleanor, but it was with Bee that he had danced first. Faced with the moment of his first dance with Eleanor, he had found something that he wanted more. He went across the room to Bee and said: 'Will you dance with me?' They had danced happily together, not speaking much. Her only remark was: 'Who taught you to cheat someone out of a race like that?'

Brat had smiled happily and said, 'I didn't have to be taught. It came naturally.'

Bee laughed and they went on dancing quietly, each enjoying the other's company. She was a lovely woman, Bee Ashby, and he loved her. The only other person he had loved was a horse called Smoky.

'I haven't seen much of you this afternoon,' said Eleanor. Brat said that he had wanted to talk to her before the race but she was deep in conversation with Roger Clint.

'Oh yes. I remember. His uncle wants him to leave the farm and go and live in Ireland. His uncle is Tim Connell who has the famous Kilbarty stud. But Roger doesn't want to leave England.'

I can understand that, Brat thought. England and Eleanor together would be heaven. 'I don't see him here tonight?' he said.

'No, he didn't stay for the dance. He just came for a silver cup to take home to his wife.'

'His *wife*!'

'Yes, she had their first baby last week, and she sent him to the show to get a silver cup for it. What's the matter, Brat?'

'Remind me to break Ruth's neck,' he said, beginning to dance again.

Eleanor looked amused and said: 'What stories has Ruth been telling you?'

'She said he wanted to marry you.'

'Well, he did have an idea like that a long time ago. Maybe Ruth didn't know he had got married. Anyway, are you going to be a big brother and control my plans to get married?'

'No, no. Why? Have you any?'

'None at all.'

As the night went on he danced more and more with Eleanor. 'You really must dance with someone else, you know,' she said.

'I have.'

'Only with Peggy Gates.'

'So you've been watching me. Am I stopping you from dancing with someone you want to dance with?'

'No. I love dancing with you.'

'All right, then.'

Brat was thinking that this was perhaps the first and the last night he would ever dance with Eleanor. A little before midnight they went to get something to eat. As they were eating, Eleanor suddenly said: 'Stay still for a moment, you've got an insect on your collar.'

She reached over and hit the back of his neck lightly. 'Oh it's going down your neck!' In a rough sisterly manner she bent his head aside with one hand while she caught the insect inside his shirt with the other hand.

'Got it?' he asked.

But Eleanor was silent, and he looked up at her.

'You're *not* my brother!' she said. 'I couldn't feel the way I just . . .' She stopped, shocked. They could hear the music from the room next door.

'Oh Brat, I'm sorry! I didn't mean that! I think I must have drunk too much.' She began to cry. 'Oh, Brat, I'm sorry!' She picked up her bag and said, 'I'll go and lie down until I feel better.'

Brat let her go and went to the bar which was empty except for Simon, all by himself with a bottle of champagne, at a table in the far corner.

'Ah! My big brother,' said Simon. 'Have a drink.'

'Thanks. I'll buy my own.'

He bought a drink at the bar and carried it back to Simon's table. 'I haven't had a chance to congratulate you on your win with Timber,' he said.

'I don't need congratulations from you.' Simon was certainly drunk. 'That was very rude of me, wasn't it?' he said like a pleased child. 'But I enjoy being rude. You don't like me, do you?' He seemed pleased at the thought.

'Not much.'

'Why not?'

'I suppose because you're the only person who doesn't believe that I am Patrick.'

'You mean, don't you, that I'm the only one who *knows* you're not Patrick?'

There was a long silence while Brat stared into Simon's shining eyes.

'You killed him,' he said, suddenly sure of it.

'Of course I did.' Simon looked delightedly at Brat. 'But you'll never be able to say so, will you? Because, of course, Patrick isn't dead at all. He's alive, and I'm talking to him.'

'How did you do it?'

'You'd like to know, wouldn't you? Well, I'll tell you. I can be in two places at once.'

He sat back and enjoyed Brat's problem. 'You must think I'm a lot drunker than I am, my friend, if you think I'm going to tell you all the details. I've told you about Patrick, because you can't tell anyone else. We're in this together now, with this little secret. Partners in crime.'

'Then, why did you do it?'

'He was a very stupid little boy, and not good enough for Latchetts. I hated him, if you want to know.'

He poured himself another glass of champagne and drank it. 'It's a wonderful partnership, isn't it. Just like being twins again. I can't tell about you, and you can't tell about me!'

'You have an advantage, though,' said Brat coldly.

'I have? How?'

'You don't care what you do. I have to accept you, but you don't intend to accept me, do you? You did your best to kill me this afternoon.'

'Not my best. I'll do better,' said Simon with a smile.

'I expect you will. A person who can be in two places at once can do better than a loose saddle belt.'

'Oh much better. But I have to take any chance that comes. I suppose you wouldn't like to tell *me* something?'

'Tell you what?'

'Tell me who you are?'

Brat sat looking at Simon for a long time.

'Don't you recognize me?' he said.

'No. Who are you?'

'Retribution,' said Brat, and finished his drink.

He walked out of the bar and tried to think of some place where he could be alone to think this thing out. There was nowhere in the hotel; even in his bedroom Simon could join him

'*Who are you?*' '*Retribution.*'

70

at any moment. He would have to go out. On his way he met Bee.

'Has everyone gone crazy?' Bee said angrily. 'Eleanor is upstairs crying, Simon is getting drunk in the bar, and now you look like a ghost. What is the matter with everybody?'

'Eleanor and Simon have had a very tiring day, I expect,' Brat replied.

'And what makes you so white in the face?'

'I need some fresh air. Do you mind if I take the car, Bee?'

'Take it where?'

'I want to see the sun rise over Kenley Vale.'

'Alone?'

'Yes, alone.'

'Put on your coat,' she said. 'It's cold out.'

At the top of the hill looking over Kenley Vale Brat stopped the car. It was still dark. He got out and listened to the silence.

He had been right about Simon. Just like Timber – a well-bred creature with beautiful manners, who was also a dangerous killer. Simon had told him the truth, back there in the bar. Simon had been glad to tell him the truth. They said that all killers wanted to talk about their killings. Simon must often have wanted to tell someone how clever he had been. But he could never tell anyone until now, when he had a 'safe' listener.

He, Brat Farrar, was the 'safe' listener. Simon thought of them now as 'partners' in keeping his crime secret.

But that for Brat, was not possible. The criminal plan he had agreed with Alec Loding was one thing, but this partnership with Simon was unthinkable.

So, what was he going to do about it?

Go to the police and say: 'Look, I'm not Patrick Ashby at all. Patrick Ashby was killed by his brother, Simon, eight years ago. I know, because he told me when he was a little drunk.'

And the police would tell him that they had investigated the death of Patrick Ashby and it had been proved that Simon Ashby had spent the afternoon with the blacksmith at Clare.

He could tell them the truth about himself, but no one would believe what he said about Simon, and nothing would be changed except his own life.

How had Simon done it?

'I have to take any chance that comes,' he had said. What 'chance' had been available that day eight years ago? Something that had seemed completely innocent and that nobody would ever suspect.

Brat stayed there for hours until the first light of morning arrived. He was no nearer finding an answer to the problem that faced him.

But one thing that Simon's confession meant was that Brat could not go on with his life at Latchetts.

Chapter 14

A priest's advice

It was Thursday morning and on the following Sunday Charles Ashby would arrive in Southampton and nothing would stop the celebrations. Brat began to feel desperate.

He went into Westover and read over again, very carefully, the newspaper and police reports about Patrick's death. He discovered nothing new.

He returned to Latchetts and took one of the horses out to ride where he had gone that first day with Timber. What had looked so beautiful to him then was no longer so wonderful. That first time it had seemed perfect. Even that silly girl who had come and talked to him had not taken away his pleasure in the countryside. He remembered her shock when she found he was not Simon. She had come there because it was Simon's favourite place for riding. Because he . . . what?

Brat listened to the girl's voice in his mind.

'Because he . . .?'

Brat got slowly to his feet and looked across the valley to Tanbitches hill. He knew now how Simon had done it. And he also knew the answer to something that had puzzled him. He knew why Simon had been afraid that, somehow, it was the real Patrick who had come back.

He got on the horse and went back to the stables. He left a note for Bee to say that he would not be in for dinner and went out as it was beginning to rain.

He walked up the path to Tanbitches thinking about his new problem.

How could he bring this thing on Bee?

On Eleanor? On Latchetts?

Hadn't he already done Latchetts enough harm?

Would it matter so much if Simon was left as owner of Latchetts, as he had been for eight years?

If Simon was punished for what he had done, it would mean more and more horrors for Bee and the rest of the family.

He, Brat, didn't have to do anything. He could go away, disappear, leave things just as they had been a month ago.

What would Patrick want? If he could choose, thought Brat, he would not want Simon to be punished because that would destroy the whole family's happiness. Patrick, who had been so kind and always thought first of others, would not want that.

And Simon?

Simon expected Brat to do nothing and stay at Latchetts, twin partners in crime. Should he, could he do that? Or should he disappear and leave Simon to spend a long life as the owner of Latchetts? Should Simon's children inherit Latchetts? If

Simon was punished, there would be no more Ashbys at Latchetts.

Would it be right to protect Latchetts by hiding a murderer?

Brat had come to Latchetts by such strange ways – a chance meeting with Loding in a London street. Perhaps there was a hidden purpose there. Perhaps he had been sent in order to uncover this murder.

What was he to do? Who could advise him?

It was late that night that George Peck, listening to the rain on the window of his study, heard another sound at that window and went to the front door.

'May I come in and talk to you?'

'Of course, Patrick. Come in.'

Brat stood on the doorstep, water running from his coat. 'I'm afraid I'm very wet,' he said.

'Take off your coat and leave it here,' said the priest. 'Come through into my study and let me get you a drink. Whisky?'

'Thank you,' said Brat when he had drunk a large whisky. 'I'm sorry to come and worry you like this, but I had to talk to you. I hope you don't mind.'

'I'm here to be talked to,' replied the priest.

'I want your advice about something very important, but can I talk to you, just between ourselves, a sort of confession? I mean, without your feeling that you must do something about it.'

'Whatever you say will remain between ourselves.'

'Well, first I have to tell you something. I am not Patrick Ashby.'

'No,' agreed the priest. And Brat stared at him.

'You mean you *knew* I wasn't Patrick?'

'I rather thought you weren't.'

'Why?'

'There is more to a person than a body. The first time I met

74

you I was almost sure that I had never met you before.'

'And you did nothing about it?'

'What should I have done? Your lawyer, your family and your friends had all accepted and welcomed you. I had nothing to prove that you were not Patrick Ashby. And I thought that the situation would not continue for long.'

'You mean, that I should be found out?'

'No. I mean that you didn't seem to me to be someone who would be happy in the kind of life you had chosen. Your visit tonight suggests that I was right.'

'But I didn't come here tonight just to confess that I am not Patrick.'

'No?'

'No, that is only a part of it, but I had to tell you that first. But I'm still not clear in my mind what to say.'

'Perhaps if you told me first how you came to Latchetts at all, that would at least clear *my* mind.'

'I – I met someone in America who had lived in Clare. They – she thought I looked like an Ashby, and suggested that I should pretend to be Patrick.'

'And you have to pay her some of the money you get as Patrick Ashby?'

'Yes.'

'I can only say that she earned her money. She must be a wonderful teacher. Are you American, then?'

'No,' said Brat. 'I was brought up in an orphanage. I was left on its doorstep.' And he told George Peck the story of his life.

'I've heard of your orphanage,' said the priest. 'It's a very good one, and it explains your very good education and manners.'

'I had to tell you all this,' continued Brat, 'because of something I found out. Patrick didn't kill himself. He was murdered.'

75

George Peck put down the glass he was holding. For the first time he looked shocked.

'Murdered? By whom?'

'By his brother.'

'*Simon*? But my dear Brat, that's crazy. What evidence have you got to prove anything so impossible?'

'Simon himself told me. He said I could never do anything about it because it would mean admitting to everyone that I'm not Patrick. He knew as soon as he saw me that I wasn't Patrick.'

'When did this extraordinary conversation take place?'

'Last night, at the Bures dance. I began to wonder about Simon long before that. Last night I challenged him because of something he said about *knowing* I wasn't Patrick. He laughed and told me the truth – that he had killed Patrick.'

'I think that perhaps the situation does a lot to explain what happened.'

'You mean you think we were both drunk?'

'Not exactly drunk, but you had had more than a little to drink. And you challenged Simon about this. Simon has a strange sense of humour, and he told you what you expected to hear. As a sort of bad joke.'

'Believe me, I'm not here because of one of Simon's bad jokes. Patrick didn't kill himself. Simon murdered him. And I know how he did it.'

And Brat told George Peck how the murder had happened.

'But Brat, you have no facts to prove all that. It's a clever idea, but you can't prove it.'

'We can get the facts, if the police once know the truth,' said Brat. 'But that isn't what I want to know. I want advice about . . . whether to leave things as they are.'

And he explained his difficulties and worries about the Ashby family and Latchetts.

76

But the priest, rather surprisingly, had no doubts about this. If murder had been done, then the law must be obeyed. His point was, however, that Brat had no proof against Simon.

'I still think that this idea is something you have imagined. I cannot believe that Simon would deliberately kill his own brother.'

And that, when Brat left him at about two o'clock in the morning, was still the priest's opinion.

'Come and see me again before you decide anything,' he said, but Brat now had the answer to his main question. If he had to choose between love and duty, the choice had to be for duty.

Chapter 15

Finding the evidence

On Friday morning Simon came bright and cheerful to breakfast and greeted Brat with pleasure. He seemed to be looking forward to their new secret 'partnership'.

Eleanor, too, seemed to be back to normal in her relationship with Brat. She suggested that they should go into Westover that afternoon to have their names put on the four silver cups they had won.

'It will be nice to have "Patrick Ashby" on a cup again,' she said.

'Yes, won't it?' Simon said.

Simon was clearly enjoying the chance of laughing quietly at his 'twin'. But when Brat told Bee that he had talked late with George Peck the previous night, Simon looked up sharply with a worried look in his eyes.

When Eleanor and Brat were leaving for Westover in Eleanor's little car, Simon appeared and insisted on coming with them. They chose the letters for the cups and then Brat went off alone to do some shopping.

He had decided what to do. If George Peck, who knew all about the weaknesses of Simon's character, did not believe that Simon could have murdered Patrick, there was no hope that the police would believe Brat's story. So he was going to provide them with the evidence which would prove it.

He went down to the harbour and found a shop where he bought a long piece of rope; it was very thin and light, but also very strong. He put the rope in a box and put the box in the back of Eleanor's small car.

When Simon and Eleanor came back to the car, Simon noticed the box in the back.

'What's in the box, Eleanor?' he asked.

'I didn't put any box there,' replied Eleanor.

'It's mine,' Brat said.

'Oh, what is it?' she asked.

'A secret,' he said, but he knew that Simon was determined to find out what it was. Better, he thought, to be honest about it. 'If you must know, it's some rope. I used to be able to do tricks with rope, and I want to practise again.'

Eleanor was delighted. Brat would have to show them some tricks and then teach her.

When they arrived back at Latchetts he took the rope out and left it in the hall. No one took any more notice of it.

Late that night, well after midnight, Brat went quietly downstairs, took the rope and went softly out into the night. He made his way across the grass and sat down to make footholds at regular intervals all the way along the rope. When he had finished, he put the rope over his shoulder and walked towards the Tanbitches path. Every few minutes he stopped and waited to see if he had been followed. But nothing at all moved in the night. At the top of the hill he reached the trees near the steep side of the old quarry. Below there was only the dark thickness of trees in the depths of the quarry. Again there was no sound in all the sleeping countryside.

Brat carefully tied the rope round the largest of the young beech trees and let the other end fall over the edge of the quarry into the green darkness below. Old Abel had told him about the quarry. There was no water in it. Brat tested the rope several times and then slid slowly over the edge and felt for the first foothold. Now that his face was level with the ground he realized that the sky seemed brighter and he could see the dark shapes of the trees above him.

He had found his first foothold on the rope, but his hands were still at the top of the rope where it lay across the grass.

'I should hate,' said Simon's voice in its slow, lazy way, 'to let you go without saying goodbye. I mean, I could just cut the rope and let you think, if you had time to think at all, that it had broken. But that wouldn't be any fun, would it?'

Brat could see Simon's shape against the sky. He seemed to be half-kneeling on the edge, by the rope. Brat could touch him by putting out a hand.

What a fool he had been! Simon had taken no chances. He hadn't even taken the chance of following Brat. He had come first and waited.

'Cutting the rope won't do much good,' he said. 'I'll only land in the branches of some trees farther down, and shout until someone hears me.'

'I know better than that,' said Simon. 'A personal friend of mine, this quarry is. Almost a relation, one might say. It's a steep drop to the bottom, a long way down,' he laughed.

Brat wondered if he had time to slide very fast down the rope before Simon cut it. Would he be near the bottom before Simon realized what was happening?

Or would it be better – ? Yes. He held the rope firmly, pushed on his foothold and lifted himself until he had almost got one knee on the grass again. But Simon must have his hand on the rope somewhere. He had felt the movement.

'Oh, no, you don't!' he said and brought his foot down on Brat's hand. Brat grabbed the foot with his other hand and held on, his fingers in the opening of the shoe. Simon brought his knife down on Brat's wrist and Brat shouted, but did not let go. He pulled his right hand from under Simon's shoe and caught him round the back of the ankle. His body was on top of the rope in front of Simon, and as long as he could hold on, Simon could not turn to cut the rope behind him. It is very frightening to have your foot held from below when you are on the very edge of a cliff.

'Let go!' cried Simon, stabbing with his knife.

'If you don't stop that,' gasped Brat, 'I'll pull you over with me.'

'Let go! Let go!' cried Simon again, hitting wildly and not listening.

Brat moved the hand that was holding on to the edge of the shoe and caught the knife-hand as it came down. He now had his right hand round Simon's left ankle, and his left hand was holding Simon's right wrist.

Simon screamed and tried to pull away, but Brat hung on to his wrist. He had a firm foothold, but Simon had nothing to hold on to. He tore at the hand that was holding the wrist, and Brat suddenly took his right hand from Simon's ankle and caught Simon's left wrist with it. He was now holding Simon by both wrists and Simon was bent over him.

'Drop that knife!' Brat cried.

As he said it, he felt the ground at the edge of the quarry move a little below the grass. It made no difference to him because his foothold was firm. But to Simon, already bent over by Brat's arm and body, it was fatal.

Simon screamed and tried to pull away.

Brat saw the dark shape of Simon's body fall forward on top of him. It knocked him from his foothold on the rope, and he fell down with it into darkness.

A great bright light exploded in his head, and he stopped knowing anything at all.

Chapter 16

The past and the future

Bee sat in the dirty little café with a cup of coffee in front of her and read the sign on the other side of the road for the hundredth time in the last forty-eight hours. The sign said: MOTORISTS. PLEASE DO NOT USE YOUR HORN. THIS IS A HOSPITAL. It was only seven o'clock in the morning, but Bee was now a regular customer at any hour.

Her life was shared between the hospital and the café and she found it difficult to remember a past and quite impossible to think of a future. There was only the 'now', a dull, half-world of grey misery. Last night she had slept in a bed in the hospital, waiting for news. 'No, no change,' the nurse would say, or 'Better go out and get a meal.' And she would come across to this café, and sit and wait.

The door opened and Dr Spence, the family doctor, came in.

'Well?' she said.

'He's still alive.'

'Conscious?'

'No. But there are better signs. But we still don't know if he will live or not. I have to go back to Clare now, but don't worry. He's in good hands.'

When the door opened a few minutes later, Bee did not look up. It would not be another message from the hospital already, and nothing had any importance for her that was not a message from the hospital. She was surprised when George Peck sat down beside her.

'George!' she said. 'What are you doing in Westover at seven o'clock in the morning?'

'I've come to tell you that it is perhaps better that Simon is dead.'

He took something from an envelope and laid it in front of her on the table. It had been damaged by the weather, but could still be recognized. It was a black stylograph pen with thin yellow lines round it.

She looked at the pen for a long time without touching it, then looked up at the priest.

'Then they have found – the body?'

'Yes. It was there.'

'What – what is there? I mean, what – what is left?'

'Just bones, my dear. And some pieces of cloth.'

'And his pen?'

'That was separate,' he said carefully.

'You mean, it – had been – that it had been thrown down afterwards?'

'Perhaps not, but probably. I don't know if it will help, but the police doctor thinks that he was not alive, or perhaps not conscious, when he –'

'When he was thrown over,' Bee said for him.

'Yes. He probably knew nothing about it. Just ended quite happily on a summer afternoon. Is there any news from the hospital?'

'None. Brat is still not conscious.'

'I blame myself greatly for that, you know,' said the priest. 'If I had listened to him with more understanding, perhaps he wouldn't have tried this crazy night-time search.'

'George, we must do something to find out who he is. Oh, I know the orphanage asked the usual questions, but I'm sure we could do very much better.'

'Starting from the idea that he has Ashby blood in him?'

'Yes. I can't believe that he isn't an Ashby.'

'Very well. I'll try to get a proper investigation started. Nancy asked if there was anything she could do, or would you rather be alone?'

'Dear Nancy. Tell her it's easier alone, will you? But thank her. Tell her to look after Eleanor, if she would. It must he hard for her, having to carry on with the unimportant work of the stables.'

'Maybe looking after the needs of the animal world is good for her at the moment,' said George Peck.

'Did you break the news to her, as you promised? The news that Brat was not Patrick?'

'Yes. I thought you had given me one of the hardest jobs in my life. She was still fresh from the shock of knowing that Simon had been killed. I didn't look forward to the second part. But it was surprising.'

'What did she do?'

'She kissed me.'

The door opened and a young nurse came in.

'Are you Miss Ashby, please?'

'Yes?' said Bee, half rising.

'Oh, Miss Ashby, your nephew is conscious now, but he doesn't recognize anyone or where he is. He just keeps talking about someone called Bee, and we thought it might be you.'

For a day and a night and a day again Bee sat by the side of his bed and listened to the non-stop stream of words from the normally silent Brat. From time to time he would say, 'Bee?' and she would say, 'Yes, I'm here,' and he would go back to wherever his mind was wandering.

Outside the hospital the world went on; ships carrying relations arrived in Southampton, police reports were written, bodies were buried. But for Bee the world was only the room where Brat was and the narrow bed where she herself slept in the hospital. On Wednesday morning Charles Ashby arrived at the hospital. Bee went to welcome him and took him up to Brat's room.

'He's asleep just now,' she said, 'so you'll be very quiet,

won't you?'

Charles took one look at the young face and said: 'Walter.'

'His name is Brat.'

'I know. But that is exactly what your cousin Walter used to look like at that age.'

Bee came nearer and looked. 'You think he's Walter's son?'

'Certainly. He's got a more honest face than Walter, though. But I'd swear he's Walter's son. I hear you all liked him.'

'We loved him,' she said.

'It's all very sad. But what are we going to do about him? For the future, I mean.'

'We don't know yet if he has a future,' said Bee.

The story of exactly what had happened was never made fully public. Simon Ashby was dead and it would help nobody to say too much about his crime.

Simon, when he was only thirteen years old, had killed his brother. Then he had calmly written a note in his brother's handwriting, thrown the stylograph into the quarry after his brother's body, and gone home quietly to supper when he was chased out of the blacksmith's. Later he had gone out on his pony to help in the night search for his brother. Some time during that night he had taken his brother's coat to the cliff-top, far away from Tanbitches, and left it there with the note in the pocket.

The problem of Brat remained. Not the problem of who he was, but the problem of his future. The doctors had decided that he would live, but he would need a long time to recover properly.

'Uncles Charles came to see you one day when you were ill,' Bee said to him one day. 'He was surprised how much you looked like Walter Ashby, my cousin.'

'Yes?' said Brat. He was not very interested. What did it

matter now?

'We began to enquire about you.'

'The police did that,' said Brat. 'Years ago.'

'Yes, but they had very little information, starting from the doorstep of the orphanage. We started at the other end. Walter's end. He never stayed in one job for long, but we found that about twenty-two years ago he was in charge of a stable in Gloucestershire for a couple of months while the owner was away. There was a young girl who worked in the kitchen; she was a very good cook, but she really wanted to be a nurse. Everybody liked her and when they found she was going to have a baby, they let her stay on and she had the baby in a local hospital.

'She would never say who the father was; the owner thought it was probably Walter, but he had gone on to some other job. One day the girl said she was taking the baby home – and she didn't come back. But the owner had a letter from her a long time afterwards, thanking her for her kindness. The girl had become a nurse, she wrote, and she had made sure that her baby had been well looked after.'

Bee looked at Brat. He was lying with his eyes on the ceiling, but he appeared to be listening.

'Her name was Mary Woodward. She was a good cook, but an even better nurse. She was killed during the war, taking some patients to safety. I don't believe that Walter ever knew about the girl and her baby. He was a kind person who would have rushed to marry her, if he had known.'

Bee had another look at Brat. Perhaps she had told him all this too soon, before he was strong enough to take an interest in life.

'I'm afraid that is as near as we can get, Brat. But none of us has any doubt that you are Walter Ashby's son.'

A week or two later she said to Eleanor, who was now the owner of Latchetts.

'Eleanor, I'm going to leave you. I'm going to rent Tim Connell's stud at Kilbarty in Ireland.'

'Oh, Bee!'

'Not immediately, but when Brat is able to travel.'

'You're taking Brat there? What a wonderful idea, Bee! It solves such a lot of problems. But what shall we do about letting people know about Brat? I mean, about his not being Patrick.'

'I don't think we'll have to do anything about it. The facts will certainly leak out, bit by bit. People will soon realize that we're making him part of the family, and not accusing him of doing anything criminal. That will take most of the fun out of it for anybody who wants to make trouble. We'll survive, Eleanor. And so will Brat.'

'Of course we will. And the first time someone mentions it to me, I shall say: "My cousin? Yes, he did pretend to be my brother. He is very like Patrick, isn't he?" And I shan't say anything more than that.'

She stopped for a moment and then added: 'But I should like the news to get round before I'm too old to marry him.'

'Are you thinking of it?' said Bee in surprise.

'I'm set on it.'

Bee hesitated, then decided to let the future take care of itself. 'Don't worry. The news will get round.'

'Now that Uncle Charles is here, and is going to settle down at Latchetts,' she said later to Brat, 'I can go back to having a life of my own somewhere else.'

His eyes came away from the ceiling and looked at her.

'There's a place in Ireland I have my eye on. Tim Connell's stud at Kilbarty.'

She saw his fingers play unhappily with the sheet.

'Are you going away to Ireland, then?' he asked.

'Only if you will come with me, and manage the stable for me.'

Tears came into his eyes and began to run down his cheeks.

'Oh, Bee!' he said.

'I see that my offer is accepted,' she said.

GLOSSARY

allowance money given to someone regularly
beech a kind of tree
blacksmith a person who makes things from metal
bear *(v)* to allow something to continue when it causes pain
box *(n)* a 'room' in a stables for one horse
breed *(v)* to produce young (horses or children)
canter (of a horse) to run, but not fast
casually carelessly, not seriously
champagne white sparkling wine
charm *(n)* the ability to please people and make them like you
crush *(v)* to push something hard until it breaks
deny to say that something is not true
drunk *(adj)* feeling the effects of too much alcoholic drink
estate *(n)* a large area of land owned by one family
evidence facts which show what happened
faced with in the face of
fall for to be cheated by (a trick)
fence something to jump over in a horse race
firmly deliberately
foal a young horse
foothold a place to put your foot safely
gallop (of a horse) to run fast
give up to stop trying
grab to take something suddenly, roughly or rudely
horseshoe an iron shoe, for a horse's foot
humour (sense of humour) the ability to be amused, or be
  amusing
imposter someone who pretends to be another person

increase to make bigger

lame unable to walk normally, because of an injury to the leg

leak out to come out slowly

loosen to undo something so that it is not so tight

master the boss; an employer

mention to say

mind *(n)* the part of us that thinks, understands, remembers, etc.

misery great unhappiness

nursery a bedroom for small children

orphanage a home for young children who have no parents

partner someone who shares

pony a small horse

priest an official of the church

property something that belongs to someone

protect to keep somebody or something safe from harm or injury

quarry a place from which stone is taken, for building

recover to get well again

relax to become less anxious or worried or tense

relief freedom from fear or worry

respectable of good quality

retribution punishment sent by God

saddle a leather seat for a rider on a horse

self-centred interested only in oneself

set on determined about

settle down to decide to live in one place

silence being silent

spoilt *(adj)* looked after with too much kindness

stab to push something sharp (e.g. a knife) into something or
  somebody

stables buildings for horses

stand up to to be against; to resist

stud a farm for breeding horses

swear to say or promise something very seriously

tight fixed strongly

twins two children born of the same mother at the same time

upset unhappy, worried, disappointed

waste *(n)* doing something with no useful purpose

waste *(v)* to use to no purpose

ACTIVITIES

Before Reading

1 Read the story introduction on the first page of the book, and the back cover. How much do you know now about *Brat Farrar*? For each sentence, circle Y (Yes) or N (No).

　1　Brat Farrar looks like Patrick Ashby. Y/N
　2　Patrick Ashby was killed in a plane crash. Y/N
　3　Brat Farrar has been a criminal for many years. Y/N
　4　Patrick Ashby was rich. Y/N
　5　The Ashby family seemed pleased that Patrick had come back. Y/N

2 What do you think will happen in the story? For each sentence, circle Y (Yes) or N (No).

　1　The truth about Brat Farrar will be discovered and he will go to prison. Y/N
　2　Brat Farrar will carry on pretending to be Patrick Ashby and will be rich for the rest of his life. Y/N
　3　The real Patrick Ashby will come back. Y/N
　4　Brat Farrar will discover that Patrick Ashby didn't kill himself. Y/N
　5　Someone will try to kill Brat Farrar. Y/N
　6　Brat Farrar will kill someone. Y/N
　7　Brat Farrar will fall in love. Y/N
　8　We will find out that Brat Farrar really is an Ashby. Y/N

While Reading

Read Chapters 1 to 3, and then complete this passage with the correct names. Use either a first name, or a first name and a surname, each time.

There were five Ashby children: the twins, _____ and _____, their sister _____, and the younger twins, _____ and _____. Their aunt _____ had come from London to look after them when their parents, _____ and _____, were killed in a plane crash. Then _____, who was the oldest child, killed himself when he was only thirteen. The Ashby family had lived at Latchetts for more than two hundred years, but they were not rich. _____ had had a lot of money, and _____ would inherit this on his twenty-first birthday. But _____ earned money to keep the family by working with horses. Her friend _____, who was married to the local priest, _____ _____, used to live at Clare House when she was young. But her family had not looked after their money and in the end the house was sold. Her brother, _____ _____, became an actor and changed his name to _____ _____. He was not very successful, so when he met _____ _____ by accident in London, he saw a way of making lots of money easily. He told _____ that he could pretend to be _____ _____, because he looked just like him. When _____ got the Ashby money, he could share it with _____. So _____ went to see the Ashbys' lawyer and told him that _____ had not died when he was a child, but had run away to the United States. The lawyer thought that perhaps the story was true, because when he first saw _____, he thought that he was _____ _____.

Read Chapters 4 to 6. Here are some untrue sentences about them. Change them into true sentences.

1 After Patrick died, Simon kept all his things.
2 Patrick looked more like Simon than Brat did.
3 Brat didn't recognize Aunt Bee when she went to his room.
4 Simon's birthday party was put off until the lawyers decided whether Brat was really Patrick.
5 Simon was very happy when he heard that Patrick wasn't dead.
6 Aunt Bee was pleased that Patrick would have Latchetts because he was very sensible.
7 Brat had no doubts about what he was doing.
8 Aunt Bee went to meet Brat at the station.
9 Ruth and Jane were both unfriendly towards Brat at first.

Before you read Chapters 7 and 8, can you guess what will happen? For each sentence, circle Y (Yes) or N (No).

1 Brat shows that he knows his way round the house. Y/N
2 Simon refuses to accept that Brat is Patrick. Y/N
3 Everyone in the family calls Brat 'Patrick'. Y/N
4 A newpaper reporter wants to write about Brat. Y/N
5 Brat remembers Patrick's favourite toy. Y/N
6 Simon lets Brat ride his best horse. Y/N

Read Chapters 9 to 12 and then answer these questions.

Why

1 . . . did Sheila Parslow want to make Simon fall in love with her?
2 . . . was Eleanor surprised that Brat had been out on Timber?
3 . . . were Bee and Eleanor pleased that Mr Gates had bought Peggy a good horse?

94

4 . . . did Brat look at an old copy of the local newspaper?
5 . . . was Bee sure that Patrick had written the note that they
     found in his jacket?
6 . . . did Brat take Timber to Clare Park?
7 . . . was Simon angry with Brat?
8 . . . was Brat unhappy when he saw Eleanor with Roger Clint?
9 . . . did Brat pull Chevron back just before the end of the race?

**Before you read Chapter 13 (*Simon confesses*), can you guess what
Simon's confession is about?**

Read Chapters 13 to 15, and then answer these questions.

1 How did Brat feel about Aunt Bee?
2 Who did Roger Clint want the silver cup for?
3 Why did Simon think that it was safe to tell Brat the truth?
4 What made Brat realize that Patrick had died at Tanbitches?
5 What did George Peck think when Brat told him that Simon
     had said that he had killed Patrick?
6 What did Brat do with the rope that he bought?
7 Why didn't Simon just cut the rope and let Brat fall?

**Before you read Chapter 16, can you guess what happens? For each
sentence, circle Y (Yes) or N (No).**

1 Brat dies. Y/N
2 Simon dies. Y/N
3 Brat goes to prison. Y/N
4 Patrick's body is found in the quarry. Y/N
5 Bee discovers that Brat really is an Ashby. Y/N
6 Eleanor decides to marry Brat. Y/N

ACTIVITIES

After Reading

1 **Put these sentences about Simon's death in the right order and then join them together to make a paragraph of eight sentences. Use pronouns (*he*, *his*, *it*, etc.) where appropriate, and linking words (*and*, *because*, *when*, etc.).**

1 Brat arrived there.
2 Simon put his foot on Brat's hand.
3 Simon planned to cut the rope and let Brat fall to his death.
4 The ground moved.
5 Brat tied the rope round a tree and slid over the edge of the quarry.
6 On Friday afternoon, Brat had bought a long piece of rope.
7 Brat tried to pull himself back up over the edge.
8 Brat heard nothing.
9 Simon fell on top of Brat.
10 They both fell into the quarry.
11 That night Brat made footholds at regular intervals along the rope.
12 Simon tried to stab Brat with his knife.
13 Brat caught hold of Simon's wrists.
14 Brat took hold of Simon's foot.
15 However, Simon was already waiting for Brat.
16 Then Brat went to the old quarry at Tanbitches, listening carefully on the way.

96

2 Complete the conversation that George Peck had with Eleanor after Simon's death. Use as many words as you like.

GEORGE: My dear, I'm afraid _____.

ELEANOR: Bad news? What's happened?

GEORGE: _____.

ELEANOR: Killed? Oh no! But how?

GEORGE: He tried _____. They _____.

ELEANOR: Oh my God! What about Brat? Is he all right?

GEORGE: He _____, but _____.

ELEANOR: But why did Simon attack him? I know he was angry about the estate and the money, but to try and kill his own brother . . .

GEORGE: It's worse than you realize, my dear. Simon did kill his brother, eight years ago. He _____. Brat _____.

ELEANOR: But if Patrick has been dead for all these years, who is Brat?

GEORGE: We think that _____, but not _____. I _____.

ELEANOR: Don't be sorry. It's the best news I've ever had!

3 Brat Farrar was an imposter who learnt everything that he could about Patrick Ashby. Write five sentences about what he said and did to prove that he really was Patrick. Use these words.

children's party, hair, house, wallpaper, favourite toy

Now use your own ideas to write five more sentences about things that an imposter could do or say to prove his story.

97

4 Fill in the gaps in these sentences with *must be* or *couldn't be* and then complete them in your own words.

1 Mr Sandal thought that Brat _____ an Ashby because _____.

2 At first, Aunt Bee thought that Brat _____ Patrick because _____.

3 Simon knew that Brat _____ Patrick because _____.

4 Eleanor thought that Brat _____ her brother because _____.

5 George Peck thought that Brat _____ Patrick because _____.

6 Uncle Charles thought that Brat _____ Walter's son because _____.

5 Fill in the gaps in this paragraph with words from the story connected with horses.

When Brat arrived at Latchetts, Bee took him to the _____ to see the horses in their _____. Eleanor and Bee trained the horses and also taught people to _____. They were very interested in _____ horses too, and when Brat arrived, the first _____ of the year had just been born. Brat loved horses and was pleased that he was going to be the owner of a _____. Simon let him ride a beautiful horse called Timber, but he didn't tell him how dangerous Timber was. Brat found out when he _____ towards an open gate and Timber tried to crush his leg between the _____ and the fence. Luckily, Brat had plenty of experience, and he wasn't hurt. Later, he showed the _____ that he knew how to make _____. And he won a _____ at the Bures show on one of Bee's horses.

6 **Match these words and phrases with the four twins (some of them may be used for more than one person). Then write two short paragraphs beginning with these words.**

Ruth and Jane looked exactly the same but _____.
Patrick and Simon were very different _____.

a clean dress	a great sense of responsibility
loved horses	sensible
old clothes	selfish
quiet	dangerous, like Timber
serious	bored by horses
interested in people	a pony called Fourposter
money-conscious	no real feeling for horses
friendly	bird-watching

7 **Do you agree (A) or disagree (D) with these statements? Explain why.**

1 Brat was a criminal who tried to steal the Ashby money and so he should go to prison.

2 Alec Loding was also a criminal and he should be punished too.

3 Bee and Eleanor should have sent Brat away when he left hospital, not accepted him as part of the family.

4 Brat's mother was wrong to leave him at the orphanage so that she could become a nurse.

5 Brat should have gone away without saying anything when he found out the truth about Simon.

6 It was better for Simon Ashby to die than for him to be arrested as a murderer.

ABOUT THE AUTHOR

Josephine Tey was born in the Highlands of Scotland in 1897. Her real name was Elizabeth MacKintosh. She did not intend to become a writer; her family wanted her to go to art school, but she chose to train as a sports teacher instead. Elizabeth MacKintosh used a man's name, Gordon Daviot, for her very first detective story, *The Man in the Queue*, which she wrote in 1929 for a competition. She also wrote many successful plays, often about historical subjects, using this name. But for her second detective novel, she took the name Josephine Tey and kept it for her many crime stories, including *Brat Farrar*, which was published in 1949.

Josephine Tey is known for writing clever mysteries, about interesting people who are not what they seem, and where it is very difficult to guess the ending. But she is perhaps most famous for her novel, *The Daughter of Time*, where a modern detective looks back at a fifteenth-century crime. According to Shakespeare and other writers, King Richard III of England was a cruel man who murdered his young nephews, the 'Princes in the Tower'. *The Daughter of Time* is a serious piece of historical detective work, and was important in changing people's opinions of King Richard. Sadly, Josephine Tey died quite young, in 1952, the same year that the novel was published.

OXFORD BOOKWORMS LIBRARY

Classics • Crime & Mystery • Factfiles • Fantasy & Horror
Human Interest • Playscripts • Thriller & Adventure
True Stories • World Stories

The OXFORD BOOKWORMS LIBRARY provides enjoyable reading in English, with a wide range of classic and modern fiction, non-fiction, and plays. It includes original and adapted texts in seven carefully graded language stages, which take learners from beginner to advanced level. An overview is given on the next pages.

All Stage 1 titles are available as audio recordings, as well as over eighty other titles from Starter to Stage 6. All Starters and many titles at Stages 1 to 4 are specially recommended for younger learners. Every Bookworm is illustrated, and Starters and Factfiles have full-colour illustrations.

The OXFORD BOOKWORMS LIBRARY also offers extensive support. Each book contains an introduction to the story, notes about the author, a glossary, and activities. Additional resources include tests and worksheets, and answers for these and for the activities in the books. There is advice on running a class library, using audio recordings, and the many ways of using Oxford Bookworms in reading programmes. Resource materials are available on the website <www.oup.com/bookworms>.

The *Oxford Bookworms Collection* is a series for advanced learners. It consists of volumes of short stories by well-known authors, both classic and modern. Texts are not abridged or adapted in any way, but carefully selected to be accessible to the advanced student.

―――――――――――――――

You can find details and a full list of titles in the *Oxford Bookworms Library Catalogue* and *Oxford English Language Teaching Catalogues*, and on the website <www.oup.com/bookworms>.

THE OXFORD BOOKWORMS LIBRARY
GRADING AND SAMPLE EXTRACTS

STARTER • 250 HEADWORDS

present simple – present continuous – imperative –
can/cannot, must – *going to* (future) – simple gerunds …

Her phone is ringing – but where is it?

Sally gets out of bed and looks in her bag. No phone. She looks under the bed. No phone. Then she looks behind the door. There is her phone. Sally picks up her phone and answers it. ***Sally's Phone***

STAGE 1 • 400 HEADWORDS

… past simple – coordination with *and*, *but*, *or* –
subordination with *before, after, when, because, so* …

I knew him in Persia. He was a famous builder and I worked with him there. For a time I was his friend, but not for long. When he came to Paris, I came after him – I wanted to watch him. He was a very clever, very dangerous man. ***The Phantom of the Opera***

STAGE 2 • 700 HEADWORDS

… present perfect – *will* (future) – *(don't) have to, must not, could* –
comparison of adjectives – simple *if* clauses – past continuous –
tag questions – *ask/tell* + infinitive …

While I was writing these words in my diary, I decided what to do. I must try to escape. I shall try to get down the wall outside. The window is high above the ground, but I have to try. I shall take some of the gold with me – if I escape, perhaps it will be helpful later. ***Dracula***

STAGE 3 • 1000 HEADWORDS
... should, may – present perfect continuous – *used to* – past perfect –
causative – relative clauses – indirect statements ...

Of course, it was most important that no one should see
Colin, Mary, or Dickon entering the secret garden. So Colin
gave orders to the gardeners that they must all keep away
from that part of the garden in future. ***The Secret Garden***

STAGE 4 • 1400 HEADWORDS
... past perfect continuous – passive (simple forms) –
would conditional clauses – indirect questions –
relatives with *where/when* – gerunds after prepositions/phrases ...

I was glad. Now Hyde could not show his face to the world
again. If he did, every honest man in London would be proud
to report him to the police. ***Dr Jekyll and Mr Hyde***

STAGE 5 • 1800 HEADWORDS
... future continuous – future perfect –
passive (modals, continuous forms) –
would have conditional clauses – modals + perfect infinitive ...

If he had spoken Estella's name, I would have hit him. I was so
angry with him, and so depressed about my future, that I could
not eat the breakfast. Instead I went straight to the old house.
Great Expectations

STAGE 6 • 2500 HEADWORDS
... passive (infinitives, gerunds) – advanced modal meanings –
clauses of concession, condition

When I stepped up to the piano, I was confident. It was as if I
knew that the prodigy side of me really did exist. And when I
started to play, I was so caught up in how lovely I looked that
I didn't worry how I would sound. ***The Joy Luck Club***

The Riddle of the Sands

ERSKINE CHILDERS

Retold by Peter Hawkins

When Carruthers joins his friend Arthur Davies on his yacht *Dulcibella*, he is expecting a pleasant sailing holiday in the Baltic Sea. But the holiday turns into an adventure of a different kind. He and Davies soon find themselves sailing in the stormy waters of the North Sea, exploring the channels and sandbanks around the German Frisian Islands, and looking for a secret – a secret that could mean great danger for England.

Erskine Childers' novel, published in 1903, was the first great modern spy story, and is still as exciting to read today as it was a hundred years ago.

The Accidental Tourist

ANNE TYLER

Retold by Jennifer Bassett

Everyday life in Baltimore, USA, is full of problems – getting the washing done, buying groceries and dog food, avoiding the neighbors . . . After the death of his son and the departure of his wife, Macon's attempts to run his own life become increasingly desperate – and more and more odd.

Meanwhile, he has to get on with his work, writing tourist guides for business people. Then his dog Edward starts to bite people, and he has to send for Muriel, the dog trainer. And day by day, Macon's life gets more and more complicated.